JOYTIME KILLBOX

Joytime Killbox

STORIES

BRIAN WOOD

AMERICAN READER SERIES, NO. 33
BOA EDITIONS, LTD. • ROCHESTER, NY • 2019

First Edition
19 20 21 22 7 6 5 4 3 2 1

For information about permission to reuse any material from this book, please contact The Permissions Company at www.permissionscompany.com or e-mail permdude@gmail.com.

Publications by BOA Editions, Ltd.—a not-for-profit corporation under section 501 (c) (3) of the United States Internal Revenue Code— are made possible with funds from a variety of sources, including public funds from the Literature Program of the National Endowment for the Arts; the New York State Council on the Arts, a state agency; and the County of Monroe, NY. Private funding sources include the Max and Marian Farash Charitable Foundation; the Mary S. Mulligan Charitable Trust; the Rochester Area Community Foundation; the Ames-Amzalak Memorial Trust in memory of Henry Ames, Semon Amzalak, and Dan Amzalak; the LGBT Fund of Greater Rochester; and contributions from many individuals nationwide. See Colophon on page 132 for special individual acknowledgments.

Cover Design: Sandy Knight
Interior Design and Composition: Richard Foerster
BOA Logo: Mirko

Library of Congress Cataloging-in-Publication Data

Names: Wood, Brian, 1982– author.
Title: Joytime killbox : stories / Brian Wood.
Description: First edition. | Rochester, NY : BOA Editions, Ltd., 2019. | Series: American reader series no. 33 |
Identifiers: LCCN 2019021033 | ISBN 9781942683919 (paperback) | ISBN 9781942683926 (ebook)
Classification: LCC PS3623.O6234 A6 2019 | DDC 813/.6—dc23
LC record available at https://lccn.loc.gov/2019021033

BOA Editions, Ltd.
250 North Goodman Street, Suite 306
Rochester, NY 14607
www.boaeditions.org
A. Poulin, Jr., Founder (1938–1996)

For Katie

Contents

III
LOVERS

I
STRANGERS

WHAT TO SAY TO A CHILD IN THE SPEEDWAY BATHROOM

I was midstream when this kid took the urinal on my right. There were three empty spaces, but he bellied up right next to me. Something about him, about having him so close to me there, made me uneasy. And I did not like feeling that way in the bathroom.

He was a little guy, no more than four or five by the looks of him. His waist barely topped the urinal. When he got there he rolled his pants and underwear all the way to the floor. He pulled up his shirt and tucked it under his chin. Half-naked, he leaned back and held himself. He looked like a cherub arching a stream into a fountain. But after he finished he didn't get dressed. He stood there with his dungarees bunched around his shoes and seemed happy enough to stare at me while I went. I began to wonder where his parents were. Somebody should have been here looking after him, keeping him from behaving like this.

The boy tweaked his brow. He looked at me like he was the first person to discover fire, as if this encounter had changed his view of the world. Eyes all wide. His mouth amazed at the sight of the unthinkable. I tried to lean away from him but there was no escaping without hitting the floor.

Those big boy eyes. They made me want to scold him. I mean, I really wanted to set him right. But it was just me and the half-naked boy in the restroom, and I wasn't sure what I was allowed to say. That's how it goes these days. This *what-can-I-say-here* feeling cripples me more than I'd like to admit.

Sometimes, like when I'm at the grocery store, it'll bear down on me. I'll be standing in the baking aisle looking at the bags of sugar or something, and it's pretty obvious I'm making up my mind, when an old lady slides her cart in front of me. She even glances at me over her shoulder. "Lady," I want to tell her. "You can't just park in front of people." But then I wonder if it even matters. She's probably been doing it for years. And it's not like it kills me if I sit there a moment. So I end up waiting, this vacant look on my face, as I watch her calculate which bag of sugar is the best deal. And as I gaze down the aisle I feel some strange kind of weight pressing in, like the world is too full for manners anymore.

I wasn't going to talk to the boy. But I had to do something. I could feel him breathing on it. So I gave myself two exaggerated shakes before zipping up. That's how you do it, I said without saying it. He looked down and wiggled. He tugged on his pants and his chubby fingers wiped at his thighs. Good enough. I made sure he was looking before I took a step back and flushed. The boy watched but didn't move. I cleared my throat. He startled but kept his eyes on me. I bent my head toward the handle of the urinal. I cleared my throat again.

The boy rocked to his toes. Best as he could, he stretched for the handle. He huffed through his nose and tried again. There was a resolve in this boy that I was beginning to like. The kid was determined. I could see his mind working as he looked up at the handle. He bit his lip and clasped onto the rim of the urinal. The sight of him cleaving barehanded to that filthy toilet made my neck sweat. He hoisted himself up to the flusher. He tugged the lever and the water sprayed on his body. The boy jumped back in delight. He clapped his hands as if he'd just ridden a slide and was ready for more.

Before he could go again I grabbed him under his arms. His shirt was soaked with toilet water. I took him to the sink and I brought my knee under him just as my father had done with me. He sat on my thigh and leaned for the faucet. "Don't touch," I told him. "Soap them up. Here, like this." I guided his hands to the dispenser. I turned on the water and cupped it in his palms. As I showed him how to rub his hands together, he watched me in the mirror. "Perfect. Just like that," I said. "Front and back. Bubbles all over." We rinsed our hands and I showed him where to throw his paper towel. Then I knelt down and cleaned the water from his face. I dabbed his shirt dry. "There you go. All set."

He looked down at his shirt, pulled at it with his fingers, then looked up at me. His eyes were bigger than before. Now full and earnest. And I thought he might want to tell me thanks but wasn't sure how.

"It's okay," I said. "It's not your fault." I stood and the boy jerked backwards. He held his thumb with his hand and he pulled his arms close to his belly. I spoke to him with a tone that would calm a horse. "Listen," I said. "You need to learn this. You can't stare. Not in the bathroom. Not here." I waved my hand in the vicinity of my groin. He stood there holding his thumb. "This is private. You need to respect that. Okay, champ? Got it?" I'm not sure why, perhaps my little league coach had done it to me, but I reached out and scuffed his hair. This touch jolted something in the boy. He looked at me like a snared animal. Eyes glazed with fear, a rope of spit hanging from his teeth. The start of a scream wavered in his throat.

"No, no," I said. "I didn't mean anything. There's no need for that."

The boy hollered. The veins on his temple flooded

and he bolted for the door. Even after he vanished, his cry rang off the tiles.

I didn't move. I could hear the boy sobbing outside. In two deliberate syllables he yelled *Stranger!* over and over like a car alarm. A woman asked him what was wrong. I heard her voice plunge with concern. She begged the child to tell her what happened in there.

What could I say? I touched him. I was only cleaning the boy. I was showing him how it's done.

Nothing sounded right. So I planted myself in front of the sink. I straightened my shirt in the mirror and I swept the hair from my face. I was relieved to be there alone. But the moment was dashed by a rumble at the door. His mother called for me to come out and by god she'd have it. But I didn't answer. As she wailed at the door I stared deeper into my face. I thought of that old lady at the grocery. Acting all sweet and brittle. The nerve she had, wedging her way in front of me to buy a bag of sugar.

JOYTIME KILLBOX

His Joytime Ambassador highlighted several lines of the contract. As he explained each section he pointed to them with the cap of his marker.

"In the unlikely event of death Joytime Entertainment LLC is in no way responsible or liable. By initialing here, here, and here," he slid the contract across the desk, "you hereby waive all rights for legal action and forfeit all rights to financial gain."

He was good at this legal kind of speak. The way he glossed over it all reminded Gregory of the way an announcer would blur through the contest details at the end of a radio commercial. Gregory's Joytime Ambassador looked the part too. White short sleeve shirt. A thick tie loose on his neck. The smell of burnt coffee on his breath.

Gregory moved his finger down each line of the contract before saying, "And life insurance?"

"Waived."

"What about burial costs?"

"If you'd let me finish before you asked questions."

"Of course." Gregory slunk back in the chair. "Sorry."

The Joytime Ambassador waited for him to sit still before he continued. He adjusted his glasses and read from the binder. "For an additional $10.95 we can offer you a burial rider. Our burial rider provides full clean-up, removal, and rites for your body, regardless of religious or cult affiliation," his voice lowered, "in the unlikely event of death."

"Cults?" Gregory said.

"We get all kinds." The Joytime Ambassador took

a sip from an exceptionally small styrofoam cup. "Let's see." He wiped between his lips with the side of his hand. "This covers up to but not exceeding six thousand in burial fees, including disposal tax, stationery, and program fees. However this does exclude all florals, parlor rentals, and makeup fees—as the mode of death will most certainly prevent viewings of any kind. Would you like to ensure the financial security of your loved ones by signing up for our burial rider?" The Joytime Ambassador looked up from his binder. His eyes fixed on Gregory's. He already knew what Gregory would say but was legally obligated to wait for him to find the words himself. The Ambassador tapped his marker on the desk.

"No," Gregory said.

"Excellent."

"Unless you think it'll, you know, go off."

The Ambassador exhaled slow and loud enough to steal Gregory's attention. "It's been a while. But it is a Joytime year." He rolled his eyes toward the ceiling. "And between you and me, there's not much to bury if it does."

Gregory swallowed. "I think I should get it. I mean, not for me, but just in case."

"Sure, yeah, here," the Ambassador said. He slid his pen across the table. "Check that box before you sign." He took another sip from his coffee. "I'll need your card again."

•   •   •

Along the outside of the building Gregory waited. It had been an hour, and somehow after all that time, he still seemed to be in the back of the line. Even in this, the Joytime Killbox held a kind of magic for Gregory. As each person entered the warehouse and he took another step toward the threshold of riding, an incremental growth of anticipation burrowed into his gut. He watched another man disappear behind the door. By his count the total ride time was no more than sixty seconds. About forty seconds to get situated in the box and the rest of the way with the light on. He counted the people in line as he took another step forward. Just a few more minutes now. Gregory forced himself to swallow. He couldn't get his breakfast to settle. And although he had already gone, he felt a ceaseless urge to go to the bathroom. Nerves, he thought. Nothing but anxiety. It'll pass.

In front of him was a little girl and an old man. The girl wore a Catholic school girl's uniform and her book bag sheathed her from her shoulder to thighs. As far as he knew the two had not spoken to each other and he assumed they had not come here together. Of course they hadn't. Riding the Killbox, Gregory couldn't think of a more inappropriate outing for a grandfather and granddaughter. But there was something unnerving about seeing the young girl. He had heard reports of the volume of youth who had been riding. But from the comfort of his living room chair he had shrugged it off as kids looking for a thrill. Seeing it in the flesh was different. It filled Gregory with a deep, parental fear.

"Is this your first time?" he said.

She looked up at him but said nothing.

Gregory buried his nerves. He feigned a confidence he usually reserved for a job interview. A dumb smile pulled at his face. "Have you done this before?"

She leaned her head to remove something from her ear. "Me?"

"I was asking—"

"I heard you." She put the earpiece back in her head.

"You should relax a little. Stop acting like it's your first time."

"Sorry. I was only being polite."

"Look down the line. See the focus? See them talking? No. They're getting prepped to ride. Only first timers get all chatty in line. 'What's it like? Is it scary?'"

"I didn't say that."

"You didn't have to. I'm a kid. I'm not stupid." She folded her arms as if she was playing dress-up, reenacting a gesture she saw on television.

"Excuse me. Where's that come from?"

"Just chill and get ready for the light."

"You're the one that needs to chill. I'm ready. You just chill."

"Go troll a chat room. You're not ready for the Killbox." The girl turned toward the entrance. She swiped at her phone and Gregory could hear the crackle of music pulse from her head. He knew she wanted their conversation to end. And it was best not to agitate such an energetic youth. But Gregory couldn't let it rest. How could she know he wasn't ready? A child. He leaned in and spoke loud. "Listen. I wouldn't have come here by myself if I wasn't."

She dismissed him with an exhale and focused on her phone. "You have no idea what you're in for."

"I've read plenty."

"Well, I've ridden it. So there's that."

"Was that so hard? Why are you so upset?"

"Oh, no," she said. "Look out. The line's moving. Get ready to die. We're going to die now."

Gregory tried to laugh but only a strange grunt escaped his throat. "Right. It's unlikely."

"And still somebody wins the lottery. You bought that stupid rider, didn't you?"

"Please."

"From here we're about," she pointed at the door with her phone, "twenty minutes out. Which means you've got cotton mouth and sweat soaking into your pants. Which is weird because it's so unlikely anything will happen."

The old man next to her put his hand on the girl's shoulder. He was a thin, dapper man who cast a pole of a shadow on the pavement. His fingers arched like spider legs. She shrugged off his hand. "Gross. Creeper."

"Be kind," the old man said. His voice was weak but still carried with it a grave authority. "It was once your first time too." He glanced at Gregory. "Why don't you trade me places? I'm in no hurry." He ushered the girl in front of him. "I do apologize."

"It's best I get hip to it," Gregory said. "They'll run it all soon enough."

The old man gave a single nod. He adjusted the sleeves of his tweed jacket. It was a beautiful coat from a lost decade. Wide peak lapels with a matching vest underneath, a period piece fit for waiting on a locomotive platform or the clubhouse of a horse track. It wouldn't have surprised Gregory to find the chain of a pocket watch drooping from his vest.

"My father's favorite suit was just like that when I was growing up," Gregory said. "Said it brought him luck. He was married and buried in it." The old man briefly met eyes with him, and it occurred to Gregory that he may have crossed a line. The man himself was close to death. But beyond that Gregory considered that mentioning death was taboo here. He quickly backed out of it. "I mean he didn't go out, not anything like this." His hand wheeled the air. "All natural. Nothing that could be helped, really."

"My condolences."

"It was long ago."

"But she was right. You ought to prepare yourself now." He extended a finger toward the door. "Many find it difficult to take an inventory of things inside."

Another entered and they shuffled closer to the door. Before it closed Gregory caught what he believed to be the trailing echo of a woman's scream. He tried to take a breath but found his lungs bricked over. He did not want to be there. But he did not want to leave the line in front of all these strangers.

If he weren't so terrified, Gregory might have been amazed at the simplicity of the Killbox. This phenomenon, which had shrouded the city in the mystery of terror, could have been assembled in his garage. The box sat atop a pedestal like a prized jewel. No matter where you stood there was a clean view. The walls and ceiling were formed from clear acrylic sheets, the corners caulked with a clear silicone. It was formed into a perfect cube, just tall enough for an average man to stand inside. With arms extended, one could easily touch all four walls and the ceiling. Inside, a single chair was bolted to the floor facing a square tile on the opposite wall. It appeared as if one was to sit in the chair and stare at the dark reflective square. The tile was attached to a black box that protruded about a yard, it seemed to him, outside the wall of the Killbox. From the black box, a coil of black wires twisted out of sight into the rafters. The long line of riders circled in toward the Killbox. No cry or twisted face deterred them. They were drawn quietly to the center of the warehouse.

"Oh, God." Gregory veiled his nose with a hand. He watched as an attendant carried an invalid out of his wheelchair and up the steps of the box. "They're going to let him ride?"

The old man's eyes seemed to hide deeper in his skull in the dark of the warehouse. Gregory could not tell if the old man was looking at him. "He signed the waiver. Joytime doesn't make any distinction. So long as you sign and pay." The old man pointed toward the gleaming box. "Don't turn away yet," he said. "You shouldn't miss this part."

On the far wall of the box the attendant strapped the man's locked body into the chair. His ankles were bound to the front legs; his torso fastened around the dowels of the backrest. The attendant exited and secured the door. The man was alone on the stage. His head slumped on his shoulder and his arms pulled tight against his chest. His face distorted into a cavernous frown and he began to cry.

Gregory's chest surged. "Are they electrocuting him? It looks like it's shocking him."

The little girl turned to Gregory. "Serious?"

"He's in agony. This wasn't in the waiver."

"You have no idea how this works."

"Not all react the same," the old man said. He chewed at his cheeks. "This isn't unheard of though. This is the part that's never reported. Screams, the occasional incontinence. Only a rider knows this."

"The light's not even on yet," the girl said. "That's when the real fun begins. This guy's going to totally pop. I'll put money on it. You watch."

Gregory's lungs shrunk. His heart flexed tight and he felt himself grow sick. He looked for an exit.

"You can tell he's a noob," the girl said.

"Me?"

"That guy. Look at him. He's trying to wiggle out of the chair. I don't know why he's yelling to get out." She made a falsetto voice. "*Help me. Oh, God. Help me.* Like that's going to work."

"They won't let you exit," the old man said. "Once you're in you must ride. Never an exception."

"Get ready." The girl rocked to her toes. Her nose pointed up toward the Killbox. "Here she comes."

Gregory grabbed his shirt collar. The old man handed him a handkerchief from his breast pocket. "I'm alright," Gregory said.

"You know the best part of a wedding, my favorite part?"

"No," Gregory said.

"When the bride is revealed."

"Of course," Gregory said. His eyes focused on the black box. The wires began to pulse to life.

"Most look back—of course they do. She's beautiful and they want to see the dress."

"The box. It's shaking. Is that supposed to happen?"

"Completely normal." The old man put a hand on Gregory's back. He extended his other arm toward the rider. "When everyone rises to watch the bride I like to turn the other way. I watch the groom. The way a man looks when he sees his bride for the very first time. What it does to him. All that emotion on display. You rarely see that in a man. The way he fights to hold it together as his eyes well over. That's the best part."

The tile slid up and there was a momentary quiet that stilled the line.

"It's moving. Look," Gregory said.

The girl jumped and stretched her neck. "Yes. Here we go."

Gregory held his breath. The pulse in his neck pounded his head forward. His heart quickened as he watched the box give birth to a sleek rod. From the darkness the barrel of a shotgun glinted inside the Killbox. The gun slipped into the room until it settled just short of the man's chin. The man's cheeks puffed and he snorted from his nose. He jerked his head violently to the side in an effort to avoid the barrel, but the restraints held. His chest tugged and he began to pant in quick, sharp cries. His eyes and nose ran. Horror gargled from his throat.

"My God," Gregory said. He grabbed the old man's sleeve. "I don't think I can watch."

"That'll be you soon enough," the girl said. She cupped her hands against her mouth. "Come on, man," she said. "Ride hard or go home."

The old man took a gentle hold of Gregory's wrist. "You shouldn't miss this. Look, there. It's just now starting." He guided Gregory's view to the Killbox.

The warehouse lights dimmed and the Killbox gleamed like a precious stone in a store window. A hush settled the room. The little girl held out her hand and began to count on her fingers. As she got to five a buzzer chirped and a timer lit up above the Killbox. A red light triggered and the Killbox was bathed in an ominous glow.

A roar crashed through the warehouse. In unison the riders counted down the numbers of the timer. "Nineteen. Eighteen. Seventeen."

"Now it's live," the old man said. "No safety with the light on."

Although he had barely entered the warehouse, the pedestal in the center of the room offered him an unobstructed view of the rider. Gregory winced. He did not want to witness this. He was not ready for the lifelong burden of carrying around something he could not unsee. A man shot. His blood slapped against the glass. But he could not turn away.

The invalid shook. His screams carried over the crowd with the fervor possessed only by a man condemned. He stretched his neck, exposing a map of sinew and veins. But his fits held no reward. The barrel stared him down the same. Gregory veiled his eyes. "Oh, God. Please, no," he said. He removed his hand and watched the timer cross into single digits. The crowd raised their fists. As the timer drew closer to its end their chants grew louder. "Look at him," the girl said. "Man, he's really going now." The invalid shook faster. His body rocked with an increasing intensity as if it were building to one great crescendo before remaining forever still. Gregory's heart thudded. His throat cinched tight and his tongue dried in his mouth. He grabbed at his chest. Please let him make it. Not here. Not sobbing in a box like this. Gregory closed his eyes. He could not bear the final seconds. The crowd pumped their arms to the beat of the timer. As it struck zero a buzzer rang out and the red light turned off. The crowd screamed and the house lights came on. With the commotion it was hard to be certain, but Gregory did not think he heard a gun blast. He was hesitant. But it could not be avoided. He opened his eyes. The invalid was alive, panting and exhausted in the box. Gregory chuckled. He began to clap with the crowd and a laughter overtook him. As it did he put his hands on his head in disbelief. He felt as if he might weep from the excitement of seeing the rider alive in there.

Two attendants carried the man back down from the Killbox. His head bobbed loosely as they installed him in his wheelchair. His clothes had been steeped in sweat. As he sat, his shoulders collapsed and it looked as if he had come from the back half of beyond. They pushed him toward the exit and the crowd cheered. If he had a hat, Gregory might have removed it as he wheeled past

him. The man looked up at Gregory. He wanted to speak
to him but did not. He wanted to know why. The man
scratched his head and smiled. "That was it." His eyes
fogged over. "Greatest day of my life right there."

Before the next rider, they sprinkled the floor with sawdust
and swept it clean. They spritzed the chair, the buckles, the
straps, and toweled them dry. Gregory was impressed with
the keen urgency of the attendants' work. It reminded him
of a grounds crew primping an infield between innings.

"So who fires it?" Gregory said to the old man.

"Nobody," the girl said. She thumbed at her phone
before nodding her head to the music.

"Guns don't just go off. Somebody has to fire them."

"Don't be stupid," she said. "That'd be murder. You
can't kill people."

"It's an algorithm," the old man said.

"You should learn some manners," Gregory said.

"From you? Please, that's unlikely."

"You could at least have the respect to put away your
phone."

She shook her head before turning her back to him.

Gregory threw his hands up. "I don't get it."

"They're just mathematical rules for a problem."

"These kids. I'd burn my hair to rip that phone from
her head."

"Best not to feed in." The old man shifted his stance.
"It encourages them."

Gregory watched them load another rider. This time,
a young mother. She had with her a pair of children in
matching overalls. They waited for her outside the Killbox, gleefully pounding on the glass with their palms,
jumping and shouting for their mother.

"This can't be," Gregory said.

"What?" the old man said.

"That woman. What is she thinking?"

"I know. Those kids lack guidance, smudging the glass like that."

"She's going to let them watch? It's disgusting."

"What?" the old man said. "Would you have her leave them in the car? It's not like it was in our day. Do that and they'll call CPS."

"But if it happens. Their noses are on the glass. They'll witness their . . . I don't even want to picture it."

"Answer me this."

Gregory watched them strap her in. As they fastened her ankles the mother waved to her children. "Look at Mommy," she said. Her hand fluttered and she blew them kisses. "Mommy's in the box. Look at your Mimi in the box."

"Would you give a second thought, say, if she were flying on business and her children watched with the same delight you see here, as her plane soared in the air?"

"That's rhetorical," Gregory said.

"Of course you wouldn't." The old man stuck the tip of his tongue from his mouth. He pinched it with his fingers. "When in truth, her children carry a higher probability of seeing their mother's untimely end there than here."

"This is different."

"Is it?"

The light came on and the crowd gave a less than enthusiastic cheer. "This is a spectacle. We're talking about a violent, awful end."

"Versus a fiery crash."

"It's a barrel to the chin. And they're right there." The children jumped for their mother. They banged their palms on the glass. "It's a load right to the face."

The little girl snickered. "Load."

"You know, for someone so cool, you take an interest in our conversation."

"I'm not." The girl turned to them. "It's a boring ride." Gregory and the old man watched the woman in the box. She paid little attention to the gun in her face, but instead waved to the crowd, her lips growing proud. The little girl pointed her thumb over her shoulder. "I've seen her around. First couple times she was a dumpster fire. It was friggin' awesome. Now she acts like it's open mic night or something. Totally dumb."

"Doesn't she care about her kids?"

"There's a welfare waiver thing," the girl said. "It's like, five bucks or something, and pays out the face."

"It's a sick type of show for her. How is she not afraid?"

"Understanding the odds. The algorithm," the old man said.

"I heard some of the youngsters at the office talk about it. Like getting struck by lighting on a clear day."

"Thereabouts."

"But it's still a loaded gun."

The attendants removed the mother. They cleaned the box and loaded another rider. The old man counted on his fingers for Gregory. "It's simple, really. The gun can go off only when the light is on."

"Certainly."

"A couple hundred thousand riders a year. That's about four million seconds with the light on."

"You're saying I have a one in four million chance of dying today?"

"Not quite," the old man said.

The girl held up her fingers, mocking Gregory. "Four, eight, twelve, sixteen."

"The algorithm is set for a four-year cycle," he said. "So once a cycle starts it will randomly pull a trigger once in that period."

"So there's a one in sixteen million chance it goes off on me."

"Nope," the girl said.

"Yes and no," the man said.

Gregory pressed his fingers into his eyes. "Just forget I asked."

Another rider entered the Killbox, a fetching young man. He wore sunglasses and stared into the barrel with a pitiless gaze, his mouth held fast in a pursed scowl. But when the light came on urine rilled down his leg. The crowd moaned.

"Look out," the girl said. She pressed toward the glass. "We got a leaker."

The old man stayed with Gregory. "All that matters is this. Whatever the odds may be, the algorithm will make the gun go off. The math demands it. And the rider must face it."

The young man's knees quivered and his hands began to shake. His face struggled to hold its expression. "The poor man," Gregory said. "I hope I'm not like that."

"One more and I'm up," the girl said. She nodded her head to a song they couldn't hear. "You watch. I'll show you how it's done."

As the man left the box he staggered past the line. The old man held out his hands and applauded. "Now here's a man who knows. Well done, young man."

Gregory watched the girl take her place on deck. An atavistic fear took his stomach. In a rush he felt himself unsettle.

"That one," Gregory said. He flicked his chin toward

the soiled youth. "That impressed you? Even I could've lost myself like that."

The old man leaned in. He took care to ensure his words slipped from his teeth to Gregory's ear. "There's never been a better chance than today."

The girl unsaddled her book bag and dug toward the bottom. She forced two pieces of bubblegum into her mouth. Gregory watched her scan the crowd as she chewed. She looked lost and alone and more than ever it occurred to Gregory that she was just a kid. She was here alone. This sad creature without peers, trying to impress some strangers she'd never see again. His fingers trembled and he hid them in his pockets.

"Why?" he whispered. He could hardly move his mouth to speak. "Just, why?"

"That man knows what I know. Something a nice man like you ought to know before you go through with it." The old man's head tilted back. He looked down his nose at the rider in the box. "Never gone this long before," he said. "Only a couple days left in this cycle. Tomorrow, perhaps today, someone has to die." The light came on, casting its bloody glow on the old man's face. And the grooves of his face deepened with black. Gregory turned away. His heart struck and he felt the thump in his ears. He watched the old man's face. There was a sharp hope in the way he watched the rider. Still and expectant. Like watching a bare horizon, waiting for news. He held this expressionless gaze. Black hollowed beneath his brow. The ridge of his nose reflected a stripe of red light. And when the timer broke to single digits the old man set his jaw and Gregory couldn't tell whether he wanted the man to live. The buzzer clanged through the warehouse.

Over the kick of the crowd Gregory could hear the girl's voice. Thick and wet with gum she said, "Zero. That's right, move him out. I'm up." She had a confidence Gregory could not understand. The folly of Catholic girls. The youthful revolt in a staid uniform. He did not know why. But he knew he must protect her. He would not let her ride.

Gregory moved forward but the old man stopped him. He clicked his tongue as he shook his head. "That's not for you to decide." Gregory wanted to call out. He wanted to tell her she didn't have to ride. But it occurred to him that he did not even know her name, so he stood there silent. The attendant took the book bag from the girl and set it next to the stairs. His hand circled her arm and he helped her onto the platform. She made her way toward the door but before passing the threshold of the box she turned. Her hair bounced as it brushed past her shoulder. She tugged one of her socks, evening them on her skinny legs. She let her arms dangle loose against her skirt. Above the crowd she looked even smaller, more frail. She was a child. Up there all alone. About to do something she couldn't possibly comprehend. Gregory saw the fear building in her eyes. A single touch, a simple act of sympathy, and she would have unraveled. Her eyes looked down at Gregory. She bent her arm and gave him a slight wave. Gregory looked to the floor. He did not want to see her there waving at him, asking for help in her way.

"She's never ridden it," Gregory said. The attendant turned her and herded her through the door of the Killbox. "Wait," said Gregory. "She can't ride." But the attendant was already inside securing her to the chair. Gregory pressed forward but was stopped by another man. "Stop," Gregory said and he flailed his arms toward the platform. "It's going to go off. You can't let her ride."

"No cutting," a man yelled. "Wait your turn," another said. And the crowd began to stir near the platform.

"Listen." The attendant shook Gregory by the shoulders. "I have the authority to open that back door with the front of your head. You take your place in line." The attendant's nose jabbed at him. Gregory shrank. "You're up third. He's on deck." He pointed to the old man. Then he held up his arm and gave a thumbs up. The other attendant raised his hand and extended his thumb and the wires began to shake into the ceiling. The Killbox came alive. The old man stood tall and soundless. He folded his hands in front of him. He held a distinguished stance and kept a keen eye on the girl, his lips slightly puckering as the gun stopped short of her head. Gregory pressed his back against the platform and slid to the floor. He buried his eyes into his palms, pressing them so tight sparks spidered out in the darkness. He heard the crowd bellow. The child's shrill scream. He wanted to pray, call out to some sympathetic god, but did not know how. "Please, Jesus. Oh, God," spilled from his mouth. Over and again he offered his manic plea, his spine waiting for the rough blast of the barrel to wake him. The crowd bellowed. They chanted down the numbers. Gregory cried into his hands. He readied himself for the sacrifice. But the amen of fire did not come. The girl finished her ride with the long blare of the buzzer. The relief brought more tears. His chest heaved and his palms slid wet against his cheeks. Gregory uncovered his eyes to find a crowd staring at him. He dried his hands on his thighs as he stood.

"Look at you," the girl said. "Were you crying?" Gregory turned to her. His face was red from his panicked bleating. She laughed. "God. You're such a noob," she said. "You were crying? You actually thought you were going to save me?" Gregory wiped his face with his sleeve. His throat shook but he had no words.

"If it helps, you're not the first." The old man gave Gregory his silk handkerchief. "She always does this. Latches to someone new, the poor orphan thing before she rides." Gregory felt ill. His head. That vice on his lungs. The curdling of his bowels. He was here for a purpose. A grave matter had brought him here. And it was just a game for her.

An attendant held out his hand to assist the girl. She pushed his arm away and hopped down the stairs. She whipped her bag over her shoulder and checked her phone.

"Why would you do that?" Gregory said.

She looked up for a beat and then was back down at her phone again.

"You let me believe—"

"Look, I need to go if I'm going to ride again before fifth period." She made her way to the exit. "But if you really want to hash it out," she pointed to the back of the line with a limp wrist. "Yeah, I've got to go." She left him there before he could think of anything good to say.

A mist of disinfectant stung the air. The crew was at task spraying down the Killbox. Gregory watched as the old man prepared. First the focused look, sharpening his eyes. Then the anticipations. His body leaning square toward the door. He was ready to ride and Gregory was timid to disrupt such concentration. He folded the man's handkerchief. "Sir?" he said. He held out the cloth. "In case you need it."

The old man glanced over his shoulder. He had a leg propped on the step, eagerly waiting the sign to move into the box. "Keep it," he said.

"But it's embroidered."

The attendants had the box gleaming and the man began to tap his foot. "I want you to have it," the old man said. "Something to remember me, all of it." Gregory stepped forward, pushing the cloth toward the old man. "Don't," the old man said. He turned toward Gregory. "Why are you even here?"

Gregory stammered. "I'm, I don't know. Why's anybody here?"

The old man fanned his fingers at the crowd. "For her it's all a game. I've got nothing left here. And you." He shook his head in disappointment. "You're not even a voyeur. You don't even watch."

"Rider ready?" an attendant said.

"Yes." The old man took the podium.

"Wait," Gregory said. The old man sighed before turning. "It's just that I'm tired," Gregory said. "Of being ignored, passed up and left alone. Because I'm too young to be with it, or I'm not quite old enough to be put to pasture yet. I don't know. But I know I just want to be part of something." Gregory could feel his chin quivering. He could not stop it from happening. "I want to be—"

"Nice speech," the attendant said. "Sir, get in the box please." The old man gestured for him to wait.

"Then watch," the old man said. "Don't turn away. Watch me ride this out." He sat in the chair the way a royal might. Shoulders back. His hands dangling from the armrest.

It hadn't occurred to Gregory before seeing him so singularly displayed in the Killbox, but the man was more than dapper. He was beautiful. And the thought of him being culled from this world in a glorious bang might be beautiful too. When the barrel revealed itself and the box illuminated in red, Gregory found himself clapping for the man. His fist, still clutching the man's handkerchief, pounded on the platform. He cheered and as the clock rode down he found his fear giving way to a spark of excitement.

The man held his noble posture. He didn't bargain or plead with the box. He didn't act brave or allow himself the blast of adrenaline. Instead he leaned his chin to the center of the gun. His head tilted back and he looked down his nose into the cold spiral of the barrel. It looked to Gregory like the old man was daring it to go off. He didn't fidget or writhe. There was no fighting the restraints or hope of escape. He didn't gnash his teeth in the face of death. No, he stared down the beast with a fearless gaze. What manner of man does this?

Gregory wanted to know him. He didn't want him to die alone in the box, his history lost with his blood. But before Gregory had a chance to plea for the old man's safety the box clicked and the light turned off. His ride was over.

With the call of the horn the door opened and the attendants entered the box. The old man's posture had changed. His head hung. His shoulders rose and slightly fell, a small gesture, not of relief, but of an unspoken failure. Quiet disappointment. He had defied the odds yet again. As the attendants ushered him out, Gregory waved the handkerchief like a flag. "My God. You made it," Gregory said. He pressed himself against the stairs. "Thought for sure you were going to buy it in there. What a ride."

The old man swallowed. His throat seized midway and he coughed into his fist. "It seems it is not my day," he said. He scowled at the mob. Somebody here would have his prize.

"Look," Gregory said, "I don't know anybody here. And it'd mean a lot if you'd stay and see me ride it." Gregory climbed onto the podium. "Don't want to do it alone," he said. "Don't really want to do it at all." He forced a sad laugh.

"I'd be honored," the old man said. "But it's not allowed. You'll be fine. Look at them." The crowd was stirring. They shouted for the light to come on, to load another. "If they can make it, you can." The old man brought his hand to his brow. He motioned as if he was tipping the brim of a bowler hat. Then he slid his hands into his pockets. "Until then," he said, and the attendants showed him out.

"When?" Gregory said. But the man was too far off to hear him. He felt a hand push at the small of his back, forcing him to walk, and with just a step he found himself inside the box. As he sat in the chair he was surprised at the cold sting against his legs. His arms tightened against his sides.

"Alcohol," the attendant said. He pressed Gregory's chest against the backrest and began strapping him in. "The spray makes everything feel freezing. Loosen your legs, please." He took hold of his ankle and bound it. "But a little cold beats—who knows what you'd catch from that chair?"

"Like what, hepatitis?" Gregory tried to lift himself off the seat, but he couldn't move.

The man was pleased with his work. "Okay, looks like we're all set."

"Wait." Gregory's arms tugged but stayed put.

"If I was in there, I wouldn't breathe through my mouth too much." He stepped out of the box and gave the wall two deliberate knocks. Gregory flinched. His chest heaved around the strap. "Good luck with the ride," the man said. With the door shut, the box was quiet. Gregory watched the man's mouth overemphasize each word through the glass. Now that he was alone there was a stillness that unnerved him. No movement to the air. The sound, quiet and dead. Gregory tried to move. His body shimmied against the chair. It held him. He looked between his feet. A drain was cut into the floor. He hadn't seen it before and seeing it now seized his mind with the thought of death. If it happened, dear God, his life would slip between his legs. And what remained—whatever else clung to the wall and arms of the chair—would simply be mopped away.

"Shit," he said. His teeth locked together. "Hey. Let me out. Please, don't start it. Let me loose. Please. Somebody?" He thrashed in the chair.

The attendant stared at Gregory. He didn't care enough to smirk. Instead he put a piece of gum in his mouth. He smacked a few times while Gregory wailed in the box. Then he held his hand high in the air, his thumb pointing to the ceiling. A whirring sound came from the black box. Gregory looked to the black tile on the other side of the Killbox. He could see his reflection disappear as the tile slid open. A heat burned in his chest. He felt a wet heat flood his eyes and his stomach caved into his spine. From the black square the gun barrel speared the air. First a small hole, no bigger than a dime, but as it thrust toward his face the barrel grew to the size of a cavern. Gregory puckered his mouth. He shook his head side to side but he couldn't escape the dark stare of the gun. Gregory shuddered. His lungs clenched in a hysteric scream. The light came on and the barrel reflected a menacing hue. A deep black-red, like blood not yet spilled from a body.

Gregory flexed against the chair. His arms torqued and he stretched his neck. But he could not hide. He puckered his mouth and tucked his chin. A feeble defense to stave off a shotgun. The barrel stayed centered on his face. Ominous. Merciless. As he looked into the depth of the barrel he took no inventory of his life. He thought not of his seventh birthday when his father took him to the sporting goods store and let him buy a football jersey, or his wedding day, his bride-to-be walking down the aisle, a veil so long she nearly tripped, and he did not think of their child, taken from them inexplicably, and he did not cry to God, forgive me, save me. His mind was empty, and he felt as though his insides, from lungs to groin, had hollowed, as though his emptiness was total and complete. And he felt the floor give way beneath him, that he might tumble headlong into the barrel. Nothing but him and the gun. Oblivion in waiting.

The light went off and the gun retracted. Gregory gasped for air. He took it in like it was his first. And as he took another he found that his shirt was plastered to his chest. Then the sound of the crowd returned in a rush. He could hear them chanting, clapping with abandon. The door was open. An attendant came in to free him.

"Did you see?" Gregory's hands came loose and he cradled his head. "That was—I had no idea." He tried to stand but his knees folded. The attendant draped Gregory's arm over his shoulder and shuffled him out of the box. Gregory gave a tired smile to the crowd. He was like a prize fighter that went the distance, staggering through the crowd with a beaming exhaustion. As they carried him to the exit he pumped his fist in the air. "It's so great," he said, before shaking into tears.

After the exit was a narrow hallway that led him to an office. Behind a desk a woman waited, a bank of monitors behind her, dozens of screens tiled up to the ceiling. They all displayed various pictures of Gregory. Him getting in the box. The barrel in his face. His fear. His anguish. The relief. Release.

"I like number four," the woman said. "Just look at that face. What a reaction."

Gregory laughed. Number four showed him from the gun's point of view, right down the barrel. His eyes clamped shut. Sweat pouring down his forehead. A deep frown cutting his face. It looked like he was passing a stone. "Classic," he said.

"We can print it and frame it," she said. "We got T-shirts, mugs, keychains."

"I survived the Killbox," Gregory read from a display coffee mug. It had a cartoon explosion with the picture of a man screaming inside the box.

"You can have it say something else. That's just the most popular."

"Can you put number four on a mug, like that?" Gregory pointed at the display.

"Give me two minutes," she said.

As he waited, Gregory helped himself to a cup of water from the cooler. He sat and thought about how nice it'd be to go into work. He'd amble through the office and into the break room, fill his mug with coffee. He was eager to place it on the edge of his desk so when a co-worker walked by and mentioned something about it, he could sheepishly brush it off, like it wasn't a big deal. He wondered what they'd say to him and what that'd lead to. He knew that mug would make things different. And he wondered if he came here again, maybe not tomorrow, but perhaps next week on his lunch hour, would he see the old man waiting in line with his hands folded, hoping to punch his ticket? And the girl, too. If he rode it again would they cross each other? He hoped to God they would. He wanted to know.

FALLEN TIMBERS

"When the impartial historian records his preservation of Fort Meigs, the reader will find a monument which no time can decay."
—Celebratory toast given July 4, 1813

Before I was old and wise enough to bury the feeling, I helped a man start a fire. I was driving home from the grocery store, two blocks past the fire station, headed toward an open stretch of road, when I saw him.

He was a sorry sight. An old man walking alone in a fierce summer. Even with the late sun, merciless as ever, he still wore a flannel, tucked in and buttoned all the way to his neck. And that made him an even sadder thing, it seemed to me. The man labored on with a tiny gas can. He swung his arm wildly to keep his balance. He shuffled along, right to where the sidewalk ended and it was only the road and the weeds.

I wasn't the type of person to stop something in motion. I didn't know why he was out here, so far from the fill-up, struggling with that little can. But there was something in the way he fought against his frailty, haunted by God knows what, that made me pull over.

I watched him in the rearview as he set down the gas can. He jabbed his thumb into the palm of his other hand. He had to force his hand open, massaging each finger. And I could tell there was a great pain he was working through. He shook out his arm, picked up the canister, and pushed on. When he came near I leaned over. I opened the passenger door.

"Need a lift?" I said.

He bent down and looked in. Me up front. The bag of groceries in back.

"I can take you as far as Waterville," I said. I waved him in.

He stood there rubbing his back a moment. "Up to Fort Meigs will do," he said. "Best put this in the trunk on account of the fumes." He filled the car with a smell of gasoline and stale tobacco. As the air conditioning recycled the scent it stung my nose like a cheap cowboy cologne. He kept a close eye on the old trees and the bones of the older houses on the roadside. He looked at the signs with a strange reverence.

"You run out of fuel?"

"No, sir," he said. "Don't drive no more." He stabbed a finger against the window. "Big battle fought over there, year of our Lord 1813." He squinted at an empty field. A Doritos bag spun a lazy circle in the weeds. "Ground drank up a lot of fire and blood there."

"You picked a hell of a day for an errand," I said. "Radio said it was the hottest of the year. Muggy too." He kept staring out the window. His silence made me feel strange. And I began to resent taking him on. "What're you looking for?" I said.

"Used to be a service station up there." He pointed to another empty patch leveled to the concrete slab. "But that's long past. Back to the way it ought to be I guess."

My nostrils widened. The fumes were beginning to make my head ache but I didn't want to let the cold air out. "What's with the gas then?"

"Like I told you," he said. "I'm taking it to Fort Meigs."

"They sent you all the way back there for gas?"

"No," he said. "I'm on my way there." He reached over

and touched my hand, which surprised me more than a simple thing like that should. "I'm a burn that thing down," he said. He looked out the window and chuckled. "About time somebody did it again." I watched him laugh. Even that was sad.

I wasn't sure how to respond. He had that sorry little gas can and he seemed determined enough. But I ignored it. I began to worry the heatwave might have gotten him. Or that he'd gone AWOL from a home or something and some men in white would come looking for him. "Fort's closed today," I said. I explained in a tone I reserved for talking to children. "They're only open on the weekdays. For kids and field trips about the war."

"Think I don't know that?" He laughed again. "I'm not trying to hurt anyone. I'm setting her back right. Besides," he shook his head, "you're talking about the museum part of it, the gift shop. It's a damned fort, son. Anybody can walk around it when they please."

We came around a curve and the fort rose before us. Perched on a small bluff, against the bend of the river, the wooden blockhouse and bleached palisades pierced the sky. How many times I'd ignored it I couldn't say. But he made it seem like a strange thing to me, a creature resurrected.

"Look, I can drop you off but you're not setting anything on fire."

"Like hell I won't." He touched my arm again before pointing at the fort. "Look at that monster. You tell me it belongs here."

We pulled into the lot. On weekends, a lap around the fort served as a quarter mile track for joggers. And when the sprinklers came on at dusk, the dogs would run through the lawn. But the heat hadn't quit. We were alone.

The palisades cast a jagged shadow on the parking lot. I followed him as he staggered around to the back of the car. He knocked his knuckle on the trunk. "I'm a be needing this." I could have told him no. What could a frail man do to me? But I knew I wouldn't. It wasn't worth fighting over. And part of me still wanted to know.

I kicked at the gravel. The cicadas paused their awful pulsing for a moment, but were back at it before there was a silence to enjoy.

"What'd this place ever do to you?"

"Watch your step." He was looking off across the river, out toward Fallen Timbers. "Right here we were conquerors." As he took in the view, the heat flushed his eyes. It looked like he might cry.

I didn't like seeing him like that. This time I touched him. A small nudge on his elbow.

"You want a drink or something?" I said. "I got beer at the store." I took it from the back seat and met him at the front of the car. We sat on the hood with our feet on the bumper. I was afraid to look at him so I looked at the fort. The staves looked like rotten teeth pushing up from the ground.

"Warm beer on a hot day," he said. "That's realer than any of those reenactors who muster here." He started to chuckle but ended up coughing instead. I thought to pat his back but he seemed to have a handle on his condition. "You know what they did with this place after the siege sputtered out?" He tilted his beer toward a rusted cannon that guarded the river.

"Abandoned it," I said. "Let nature take a turn at it."

"People slept in it for a while, inside the walls." He drew a square with his finger. "Kept them safe, I guess, from animals, other people. Tecumseh's ghost maybe."

"They ended up destroying it," I said.

"Something burned her down. But who knows?" He thought a moment and winced at the fort. "Not like it mattered much, old thing like that, its purpose all spent." As he looked on, his face soured. I couldn't tell if he was saying goodbye or good riddance.

"You want another?" I said.

He swirled his beer can. He took a long drink and wiped his mouth on his sleeve.

"That's enough sentiment." He slapped the hood and held out his hand. I didn't see much reason in arguing with him. I wasn't his orderly. And he was a man. He knew well enough.

I gave him the keys but stayed where I was. I watched him splash gas on a corner of the fort. "Let's see them build it back this time," he said. "She'll be burning bright by dusk." He looked over his shoulder at me. A sweet and toothless grin had captured his face.

I didn't have it in me to tell him there was hardly enough gas in that little canister to make a difference. He had little to give. And even if, for some reason, a part of the palisades caught, the fire department down the road would surely snuff it out if the sprinklers on the knoll didn't. Fort Meigs wasn't going anywhere.

The old man poured his righteous anger against the fence and it seemed to me as good a time as any to offer a toast. I turned my hand and let the beer spill. It fizzed as the ground drank it under. "To future fires," I said. But by the time I opened another, the flames he had started were already whimpering, that sad pulse of a fire dying.

II
FRIENDS

USS *FLAGG*

The first time I went to Boyd's house was the week after, to help his mom sell off his stuff. She had found my name in his cellphone and called me. "You keep half of whatever you make," she had said. She exhaled long into the phone. That uncomfortable breath of quiet. "I can't have it here anymore."

"Nonsense," I told her.

"I wouldn't keep a thing."

When I came over she stood by the window, looking at the lawn. A rough pour of liquor sloshed in her glass and she held it loose at her side. She offered me one but I declined. I could tell she was good at drinking. And I didn't want to embarrass myself trying to keep up with her. She stopped short of his bedroom and showed me in. The cleaning crew had removed the furniture and rolled up the carpet. They had tossed it by the side yard.

With the bed and dresser gone, and the floor stripped down to the tack strips, his room felt like a museum. What remained, mostly comic books and toys still wrapped in the plastic, he had proudly displayed on the walls. There was a curve of track lighting that spotlit die-cast figurines. He had a whole shelf devoted to limited editions. And in the corner was a tarp, covering something else the size of a coffin. It was an impressive haul. In the right circle these childish trinkets were worth a considerable ransom. I picked up an action figure I knew would fetch a few months' rent. "There anything off limits, something you want to keep?"

"No," she said without looking my way. "Nothing."

As I went to work taking inventory, I kept a running total. It had me kicking myself for not taking her original offer. And I hated myself even more just for thinking about it. Not even taking half, there'd be plenty to get a new car. Enough left over for a sofa, too. Thinking about it gave me a terrible urge to take something small, something Boyd would want me to have.

While I cataloged his things I found myself glancing over my shoulder to see if she was watching me. But she never was. Each time I stopped to look at her, I caught her gazing out the bedroom window, her eyes unsearching. Vacant. It occurred to me that until the service I'd never met Boyd's family. I had never been to his house. I didn't even know he lived with his mom. And I guess it made sense why he would hide that. A grown adult with a salary, living in a roomful of toys. Not the kind of thing you want passed around at the office.

That's how it was with us. I guess Boyd and I were friends the way most people are. We looked forward to our time together. And although we wouldn't share it, our attitudes changed when we saw each other. We'd buy each other gag gifts every now and then. And around Christmas we'd put a card in the mail. But when it came down to it, we really didn't know each other. Sure, we rolled dice together on Wednesdays after the comic shop had closed. I knew he liked playing a rogue, and wasted way too many ability points of charisma. Once a week we'd play trivia at the bar. His wheelhouse was American history. And if there was a dumb movie at the midnight theatre, we'd meet there before wasting the night over burnt diner coffee. I knew Boyd's Mount Rushmore of cinematic nude scenes, which superpower he'd pick if granted just one, how he'd order his hash browns at a Waffle House and how much ketchup he used. But as I stared at this cache of toys, I realized I didn't know a thing about him. Nothing that could explain why.

"Marcus," his mother said. "What was he like with you?" She took a drink and sneered at the lawn. "I never saw him smile much."

"If happiness was on the menu, Boyd would have ordered a salad."

She covered her mouth with her drink. A surge of laughter shook her chest. It quickly turned into a sob. "That kid hated everything."

"Yeah," I said. "It's what I liked best about him." She started to laugh again and I had to blow the air from my lungs to keep myself from welling over. I looked at a framed comic book on the shelf, *Fantastic Four #48*, *The Coming of Galactus!*, and felt like crying even more. "Are you sure?" I said. "This stuff is worth some serious money." But his mother didn't answer. She had already left to sulk in the kitchen. I was standing there alone.

Of course I wanted to honor Boyd. Like most of the shit he had neatly displayed in his room, he was a rare find. For guys like us, making friends wasn't easy. And the friends we had didn't get out much. But I kept having this rotten urge to keep some of his things. I wanted to take his stuff home by the armful. The more I looked through the shelves the worse it got. A vinyl cape Jawa with original packaging. *The Incredible Hulk #180, #181.* My God—a mint-in-box Storm Shadow. These couldn't be sold. They deserved better than that. Boyd had treated them right. They were curated, set apart. And now they'd be passed off, rolled out the door with the ruined carpet.

An anger I had buried roiled up to my throat. He had all of this, and he had me as a friend. But it still wasn't good enough for him. I could feel myself wanting to cry and I didn't know what to do to stop it. I flipped through a binder of *Magic: The Gathering* cards. I tried to guess how much a Birds of Paradise card could get. About $500, worn as it was. And it made me think about the time Boyd won us a gift card for chicken wings because we were the only team to get the final trivia question. "McKinley," he'd said. "Boom."

"You sure it's not Salmon P. Chase?" I said.

"Nope. That's the 10,000 dollar bill. It's William Mother Fuckin' McKinley. Book it." And after writing down the answer he flipped his golf pencil in the air like he'd just hit a walk-off. That might have been the happiest I'd ever seen him. And picturing it now, I knew I couldn't remember that moment as clear as I should. The sudden thought made me cry. Right there in the center of his room. A big fat nerd blubbering in a room full of toys. Boyd's mom must have heard me, because after wiping my face, I found her in the doorway again, another glass in hand. She held it out for me.

It struck me that I hadn't said anything to her at the service. "I'm sorry," I said. I took the glass. "I—I don't get it. He never said anything about this to me." I winced as I drank it down.

"His father got him most of this." She gestured loosely at the room. "After he left. He'd send them on his birthday, always with one of those expensive cards, the thick ones. He'd write 'Do not open' or 'This is not a toy.' Said they wouldn't be worth as much."

"He wasn't wrong. The box alone is worth a few hundred on that one."

She seemed to interrogate the wall but couldn't find what she wanted. "What's the point? Hanging on to something you can't even hold." She picked up a comic and scoffed at the cover. "Books you can't open. Can't even read. What's the use in that?"

I wasn't sure she wanted a response from me. And it wouldn't have mattered because I didn't have an answer. I just knew I didn't want his things belonging to some stranger. I didn't want the burden of knowing I shipped it all off to some poor fool trying to regain his past. I set the empty glass on the windowsill. The day had started to cloud and it looked like a rain might come. "I've got most of it written out," I said. "I'll come back to take photos. But it might be a few months for it all to go. Takes a special kind of buyer for this stuff." I pointed to the tarp in the corner. It still concealed some part of him from me. "Did Boyd keep it like that?" I said his name without weight, as though I expected him to come back from an errand.

"Cleaners left it that way. Feel free," she said. "You can look."

What I would find I wasn't sure. I might have been better off not knowing. But in remembrance of my friend Boyd, I looked under the tarp anyway. I took care folding it back, holding my breath as if peeling gauze off a skinned knee. Hiding under the tarp, coming into light in all its splendid glory, Boyd had the mother of them all, the USS *Flagg* aircraft carrier play set. In 1985 it was the biggest, best toy a kid could ever wish for. I had never seen one in person. Nobody in my neighborhood could afford one. And seeing it now made me feel like I had just encountered a celebrity. I wanted to take a picture with it to prove it was real.

Boyd had it displayed atop a long folding table. Stern to keel she was seven and a half feet. The deck housed a few dozen soldiers, three Skystriker Combat Jets, and a

Dragonfly Assault Copter. There were movable gun turrets and a fully operational winch off the back. The paint was perfect, all the decals flawless. Under the table he even had the pristine original packaging. And on the observation deck he had the Admiral Keel Haul action figure. There he was in his maroon bomber jacket, a thick mustache painted on his lip.

I picked up the admiral by the waist. "This is incredible. This guy here, version one, you couldn't buy him. You only got him if you bought the *Flagg*." I held him out for her to see.

She didn't seem to care, glancing at him only briefly. "Looks like Freddie Mercury in a sailor hat."

I started to laugh again. Boyd and I had joked about how most of the action figures of our childhood looked like pedophiles. With his sky blue shirt only half buttoned beneath his jacket, the admiral was no exception. And that made me feel like I might bawl again if I didn't get a handle on things. "When did he get this?" I said. "It's so big. I mean look at the size of the box." She was twisting the ends of her hair as she watched the clouds bundle together outside. She stopped only to fan her hand at the *Flagg*.

"A month, maybe. Had to throw out a nightstand and put his computer on the floor just to make room."

I couldn't understand why Boyd wouldn't have said something about this. He had a near mint *Flagg* with all the pieces. It seemed significant.

"Tell me," she said. I was still looking the *Flagg* over, making sure all the radar antennas spun correctly. "What's a grown man need something like that for?" As she spoke I found myself putting the admiral into my coat pocket to free both my hands.

"I—I don't know," I said. "Why does anybody keep anything?"

"Don't take it with you."

An icy weight calved down my spine. I could feel her looking at me, but I was too ashamed to turn. I stood straight and slowly removed the admiral from my pocket. I perched him back up on the observation deck.

"You can keep it," she said. "If you want. It doesn't matter, really."

"Oh, no," I said. "I wasn't going to take it. I just needed both hands to flip this hatch open." I was still afraid to face her. "I mean, you really shouldn't separate him from the ship anyway. Kind of kills the value of it."

"No. I mean the whole thing. The captain. The ship. You can have it."

I looked over my shoulder. She was still looking out the window, watching the rain soak into the rolled-up carpet. She never saw me put the toy in my pocket. "I couldn't, really," I said. "Even if I could, I came here in a hatchback."

"It comes apart. You could take it with you."

"And I'm kind of in a studio right now. I'm not sure where I could put it."

"It's fine. Here." She walked across the room and began clearing off the deck of the *Flagg*, tossing things into the large box under the table.

"Careful," I said. "Please. Just—don't scratch the stickers."

But she began throwing the vehicles harder. Pulling off the moving parts. She picked up a mint comic book and frisbeed it in with the G.I. Joes.

I stepped back and waited for her to finish. When she was done we both stood there and stared at the blank deck of the *Flagg*. Not saying a word until she broke the silence. "You want it or not?"

She helped me lug the pieces out to my tiny car. And I was honest when I said I didn't have a place to put it. The boxed soldiers piled to the ceiling until I could barely see out the back. The keel of it scratched against my window and the edge of the stern hit my elbow when I put the car into gear. As I went down the driveway it made me uneasy the way it all clattered. Each bump in the road, the value tanking a little more. At the end of the driveway I stopped and tried to readjust the *Flagg*. And I saw her looking at me from the house. She was standing next to the carpet, her drink held to her face. I was too far away to tell if she was sad or happy. And not knowing hit me in the stomach. I felt like I should have taken her someplace. Gone for coffee so we could talk about it. But it didn't matter even if I wanted to. With his things piled up and moored around me there just wasn't any room. For her or anybody.

BEASTS OF FLIGHT

The Birthday Gift

For his eleventh birthday, Christoph's mother took him go-karting.

He'd never driven anything before. And Christoph found himself exhilarated by the rush of speed. He liked how the ground zoomed beneath him, slowly if he looked straight, and blurring fast if he looked to his side. He smiled at how he commanded the wind with the weight of his foot. As his courage grew he pushed the accelerator harder. The engine whined and he felt like he might fly away. And although he was firmly in last place, he couldn't hide his joy as he rounded the track.

On his final lap, grinning with the intensity of a birthday boy, Christoph wrecked. After careening into a hay bale, he spun out. As he began to correct himself another driver collided into his side, rolling Christoph's go-kart. The tumbling made his arms flail. His head whipped from one shoulder to the other. Once the terrible motion ended, his left arm lay pinned, crushed under the searing weight of the machine.

Even after a regimen of surgeries, grafts, and therapy, the arm remained a shameful creature. Patches of skin looked like wet paper towel. Grooves of lost muscle eroded down to the bone, forcing his hand to hook in on itself. It cradled toward his chest. Below the elbow the arm was useless.

An executive from Super Kart Family Speedway mailed Christoph a formal letter. It was printed on luxurious cotton fiber paper, a fetching signature plumed at the bottom. The letter explained how Christoph's experience was unique. According to the executive, most children did not leave Super Kart Family Speedway with gnarled limbs. In fact, he included a pie chart showing how statistically children were more likely to be mauled by bears than suffer horrific life-altering trauma from go-karts. To show his endearing appreciation, the executive included a badge naming Christoph a lifetime MVP. As an MVP he was entitled to: unlimited laps and track time, a priority parking pass, and a commemorative drink cup (with complimentary soda fountain refills). For good measure he also included a coupon redeemable for 1,000 game tokens. He finished his letter with a postscript: "And a little secret between an executive and an MVP, use these tokens on the Skee-Ball machine. They have the highest token to ticket ratio!" Despite the executive's grand gestures of kindness, the pie charts and the parking pass and the cup and the tokens, Christoph was still angry.

He stood shirtless before his bedroom mirror. He followed the length of his healthy arm. Then he stared at his other limb. How incongruent he looked. Incomplete. He was ashamed of his body. He looked at the claw of what was his hand and remembered how it once held a steering wheel. How it once made the ground obey. Christoph stared at his frozen fingers. He told them to move. They would not obey.

A Christmas Miracle

At sixteen Christoph refused to go outside. He was tired of the stares, the way people glanced at his arm and whispered to one another when they thought he wasn't looking.

His mother decided to buy him a pet for Christmas. She thought it would help if Christoph had something to love, something living, to distract him from his handicap, from people.

In the pet store she was greeted by the distinctive smell of bird feed and hamster shavings. Walls were stacked with rodents in clear boxes, lizards bathing under heat lamps, a wilderness of dazzling fish. The animals seemed forlorn to her. They looked like forgotten trophies. She perused a shelf lined with ferret cages. She was amazed that such a slender thing could produce such a sharp odor. The store owner inquired about her visit. After detailing the particulars of her son's situation, repeating several times his loneliness, she added: "It's important he has a companion."

The owner nodded and said he had the perfect animal. "Twenty years in this business, this is the smartest thing I've ever seen. He'll be a friend for life." Near the back of the store he took her to an impressive cage that housed a small grey parrot. "Tell him a question," the owner said. "Go on. Ask him anything. I'm telling you, this bird's a genius."

She'd never talked to a bird before and this made her timid. She couldn't think of a suitable thing to ask. "Hello there. How are you?"

The bird jumped from his perch and gently clawed himself up the side of the cage. He nuzzled his beak through the bars. "Fine, thank you," the parrot told her. "Y tu?"

"See. What'd I tell you? Bird's brighter than his tail

feathers." The owner reached his fingers in the cage, fed the parrot a treat.

Indeed, she was amazed at this feat. But she was curious why he would sell a bird this unique, this intelligent. When asked, the owner glanced side to side; he leaned in. "Between you and me, I think he makes the other animals feel inferior." He tilted his hand like he was tipping a scale. "Sad animals aren't the best for business."

"Sorry," the bird said. "Sorry, sorry, sorry."

"You're okay, little guy." Through the bars, the store owner stroked the bird's head with the back of his knuckle. "Even knows when to apologize. You can see, he's a very smart bird."

She removed her checkbook and walked to the cash register. After licking her thumb, she flipped to the back of the book. Although she had received a healthy settlement and could easily afford the high price of the bird, she still felt moved to negotiate a better price. "Who shall I make this out to?"

"Aquatics and Exotics." He scratched his cheek while he watched her write the check.

Before signing she added, "Throw in the cage and you've got yourself a deal."

The store owner made a sour face and choked it. He held out his palm and nodded with reluctance. "You're lucky it's Christmas."

She made Christoph cover his eyes while she wheeled the cage into the living room. "It's an African Grey." She unveiled the parrot. "They can live to be 70."

Christoph eyed the bird. He looked at its white face and black eyes, the grey feathers that wracked his body, the flair of vermilion on his tail. To Christoph the bird seemed pretty simple for a rare thing from Africa. "That's a long commitment," he said.

His mother put her hand inside the cage. "The man at the store said these birds are as smart as dolphins, can learn over 800 words." She put her finger in front of his legs, pushed her knuckles into his breast until he perched on her hand. "Here." She placed the parrot before him.

The bird bobbed his head and sunk his beak into his feathers. He hopped onto Christoph's broken hand. Christoph tried to recoil but the hand wouldn't move. The bird sidestepped the length of the defective arm and settled on his shoulder. He polished his beak against Christoph's shirt. The bird rocked and leaned his head into Christoph's neck.

"He likes you."

Christoph smiled at the thought of having something as smart as a dolphin on his shoulder.

"Tu tu tu," the parrot said.

"Is that Spanish?"

"Si. Yup. Yeah," the bird said.

Christoph brought his hand to the bird's head and let him nuzzle his fingers. "I think he's speaking Spanish."

"The pet store said they mimic all sorts of sounds. Phones, door bells, cars." She went to pet the bird. It dodged her hand and hopped closer to Christoph. "Look at him. He really likes you."

Christoph let his smile go wider. With the bird on his shoulder he couldn't think about his damaged body. "I'm going to name him Tutu," he said.

That night he put Tutu's cage next to his bed. Christoph didn't like the thought of Tutu locked and confined; he left the door open so Tutu could roam as he pleased. That morning, Christoph woke to find Tutu balanced on the corner of the night stand, cocking his head, waiting to be petted.

One in a Million

So it goes: Christoph loved Tutu. Tutu loved the park. Christoph took Tutu to the park.

Everyday Christoph walked the promenade with Tutu on his shoulder. Christoph enjoyed their strolls. For reasons unknown to him, the park was full of other freaks with rare animals. There were invalids, veterans, and day drunks, a zoo of exotic bodies.

There was the tattooed lady with dreadlocked hair that always rollerbladed near the fountain in her swimsuit. She would skate in small circles with a python scarfed tight around her head. There was the toothless man who wore nothing but denim. Shirt and vest and USA ball cap, all denim. He sat on the gazebo steps, his iguana clawing against his pant leg. He kept it on a leash, the collar made of stitched denim.

Christoph enjoyed the spectacle. He liked how nobody noticed him. At the park no one paid attention to his arm or asked how he got his scars. Instead, all eyes and questions were focused on Tutu.

"How much did he cost?"

"Too much," Tutu would say.

"Can he cuss?"

"Hell yeah," Tutu would say.

"Make him say something."

Tutu would shake his head and the crowd would laugh.

"What does he eat?"

"You name it," Tutu would say.

So like he'd done before, after walking the length of the park, and after taking a moment to let Tutu preen in the sun and talk to the crowd, Christoph began his trip home. He stood at the street corner, waiting for the traffic signal to change. But on this particular day, unlike all the others, Tutu decided to mimic the chirping sound of the crosswalk. With perfect pitch, timbre, and volume, Tutu parroted the crosswalk alarm. Three impeccable chirps. Pause and repeat.

Christoph smiled at Tutu's accuracy with the noise. Just like the real thing, he thought. Like to see Flipper do that. He figured Tutu deserved a sunflower seed. As Christoph reached into his pocket, a blind man mistook Tutu's noise for his signal to cross. The blind man confidently stepped into the intersection, directly into the path of the Fourth Street express bus. With the impact, the blind man's body exploded into flaps of clothing and skin. A mist of blood hissed on the crosswalk. Pieces of cloth flapped in the air like dead leaves.

Tutu stopped chirping.

A crowd vultured around the fresh body. One woman kept whimpering, "Oh Jesus, Christ, Jesus," while most of the crowd gasped and held the sides of their heads. Some of them began to search the scene. Their eyes looked for something, anything, to blame.

Through the air, Christoph felt the weight of their stares. It burrowed into his belly. His breath quickened and he scratched at his damaged arm. He took Tutu from his shoulder and placed him on the edge of the curb. He walked away briskly, leaving the bird to preen its blood-splattered breast.

The Red-Faced Judge

Because a jury of peers could not be found, Tutu's judgment was biblical in its swiftness.

Presiding was the Honorable Tal Dipple. Along with his reputation for dealing spartan discipline, he was also known for his narrow-set eyes, small ears, and propensity for courtroom perspiration. Beneath his robe he wore a necktie cinched so tight it strangled his throat. It forced his neck skin to spill over his shirt collar, making his face flush with blood. Tiny-eared and red-faced as he was, he maintained the constant appearance of a wailing infant.

"You're telling me this bird premeditated Robert Martin's murder?" Judge Dipple said to the prosecutor.

"Yes, Your Honor. You can clearly see in the Wikipedia article I printed out these animals are extremely intelligent."

Judge Dipple held his readers up to his face.

"Please note that under the heading *Mimicry and Intelligence*, the article states *performs cognitive tasks*." The prosecutor took a dainty sip from a water glass. He cleared his throat. "Cognitive, Your Honor."

"Objection," the defense said.

Looking down from the bench, Judge Dipple examined Tutu. He did not like the way the bird disrespected his court. His claws wrote illiterate scratches into the lacquered table. His beak was prone to fits of squawking. He didn't like the way the bird kept hopping in circles, pecking at the lead fishing weight crimped to his leg. But most of all, Judge Dipple hated Tutu's round black eyes. He disliked how tight and focused they were, how they looked on him with objective indifference.

Nobody looks through me, Dipple thought. Not in my court. He ran his finger under his collar. "Overruled."

The prosecutor went on. "He planned the death of poor, blind Mr. Martin. How else could the impossible timing be explained? From the report, it's evident that this bird has not the mind of some feathered beast, but bears the intelligence of a dolphin." The prosecutor pointed at his temple for added effect. Then he pointed at Tutu. "He has the brain equivalent of a child. Should we not hold children responsible?"

Tutu did not object. Instead he tongued at his ankle. Tutu's attorney tried to settle him but Tutu remained nervous. He would not take his gaze from the judge.

Judge Dipple began to simmer. He couldn't recall the last time somebody looked at him like that. Eyes cold and fearless. He could not think back far enough. And this failed effort made his anger grow. Sweat collected on his eyebrows until it pulled from his face. He watched the bird bite at the ankle weight.

"Your Honor," the defense said, "it's obvious my client is under extreme emotional unrest. He was found abandoned, quivering. Covered in blood. In shock. The unfortunate accident at the park has rendered him unable to speak coherently. Look at him."

Tutu hopped and caught sight of Christoph in the audience. His head perked. "Chris-top?" Tutu said. "Chris-top?"

In the back of the courtroom, Christoph slid down in his pew.

"Help," Tutu said. He bit at his ankle weight and twitched his leg. "Help, help, help."

Christoph tore his eyes from Tutu. He dropped his head.

"Your Honor." The prosecutor removed his glasses. He raised his voice over the bird's. "Those were the same cries heard at the scene of the crime." He pointed his glasses at Tutu. "The crowd screamed 'Help!' as they ran to the slaughter stream that was once poor Robert Martin—a defenseless blind man. This sick beast is trying to relive the carnage of that day. He's trying to revisit the crime." As if to plead, the prosecutor placed his hands under his chin. "Serial murderers do the same thing."

The Judge dabbed his hot, red forehead. He mopped the sweat from his lip.

Tutu snapped his head. He periscoped his neck, focusing on a leg of sweat trembling from the judge's face. Tutu lowered his beak and leaned toward the judge with his ebony eye.

Judge Dipple was ignorant of the behavior of birds. He did not understand that in order to focus on anything in detail, a bird must cock its head. He did not know the twinkling pearl of sweat on his forehead wiggled down his face in the manner of a mealworm. He didn't realize Tutu was curious why a man might have worms on his face. All Judge Dipple saw was the excruciating intensity of Tutu's black caviar eye. This bird was sizing him up. This bird was judging him.

"Guilty," he said, as he clapped his gavel with such force that the sound block lifted into the air. "Bailiff, get this animal out of my court."

Taco Night in Pelican Bay

As a corrections officer, Hiram was accustomed to the bizarre. But this was the first literal animal to come through his cafeteria.

It was Wednesday, which meant they were serving Navajo tacos. The inmates were in high spirits. Hiram was not.

"150% capacity and they got the nerve to send me a bird," he said. "Kind of horseshit is that?"

The cafeteria cook perceived this as rhetorical and did not answer. Instead, he placed a piece of fry bread on a plate and slopped it with taco meat.

Hiram watched the bird hop into the serving line. The parrot perched himself between two food trays. His claws clinked against the aluminum bars. Tutu rocked his head up and down, eyeing the foreign food. He leaned his eye toward a pile of diced tomato.

"What do I give him?" the cook said. He wiped his hands on his apron. "He on dietary restrictions? Never fed no bird before."

Hiram let his wrist dangle over the taser on his belt. He tugged his mouth to the side. "Like I know?" If the cafeteria were a gladiator arena, Hiram was the emperor. He took pride in keeping a clean, tidy stage. Hiram rocked his weight from leg to leg. He nodded toward the right. "Give him some salad or something."

The cook shrugged and made a plate. He reached his arm over the sneeze guard and placed the food before the bird. "Here little guy. Chef's special."

Tutu hopped to the plate's edge. He ran his beak across the wet strips of lettuce. His feathers flared. He scratched at his beak.

"I don't think he likes it," the cook said.

"This look like a buffet?" Hiram said. "He takes his shit like everyone else. Or go hungry for all I care."

One of the prisoners took a tomato off his plate. He cradled it in his palm, held it out for Tutu. "Where you from partner? How'd you land in a nest like this?"

Tutu lowered his head. He eyed the food with caution.

"Here," the inmate said. He waited for the bird to take the food from his hand. "I ain't bite you. There you go. Nice, huh? You want another?"

Tutu took pleasure in the cool tomato. His feathers flattened and shined a brilliant grey. He swayed and let the inmate pet the side of his head.

"Don't fuck with my bird, Peanut. I'll bust a ruckus in your ass." Hiram flexed his hands against his belt.

"I wasn't meaning no harm, boss. He wants a tomato."

"Touch him again," Hiram said.

The inmate glanced away before leaving the line.

After swallowing the delicious gift, Tutu let out a melodic chirp. A beautiful noise floated above the scraping plates and the cafeteria chatter. Tutu pressed his head against the glass and sang. His talon reached for the tomatoes.

"Look now, see. Got him all riled up."

Tutu hopped forward. He tapped his beak on the sneeze guard. His tongue snubbed against the glass.

"Enough," Hiram said. He wouldn't stand for this childish behavior, even from a bird. "I said that's enough."

But Tutu kept on.

Hiram, the Fisher

Hiram hated animals. His whole life he'd had one pet. And even that was short-lived. When he was a child, his neighbor's cat had a tremendous litter. They couldn't give them away. Hiram asked his father for a kitten.

"Dirty filthy things," his father had said. "I'm pulling doubles to put a roof over your head. Your mother breaks her back in there, keeping it clean. And you want to invite animals into our house?" His father's mind was set.

That same week, at the county fair, Hiram was drawn to a carnival game. A kiddie pool was filled with water and seeded with a school of live goldfish. For three tickets he could reach into the pool and keep anything he grabbed. Packs of children gathered around the pool, plunging their fists, savagely punching at the water. Hiram paid the attendant and took his place at the edge of the pool. He licked his lips and rolled up his sleeve. He knelt and peered into the sloshing water. Golden fish scales glittered on the waves. He watched the fish, studied their behavior. They huddled into orange clouds; they scattered and regrouped. Hiram held his hand above the water, waiting like a hunter, holding the air in his lungs. As a milk-skinned boy splashed the opposite side of the pool, sending the fish in a feverish escape, Hiram knifed his hand in the water. He pulled his fist from the pool. He opened his hand to find two fish skittering in his palm. Two! He cupped the fish gently, like he was nesting a baby bird. He presented his catch to the carnival worker who tossed the fish in a plastic bread bag. The man filled the bag with water from the pool and knotted the top. He held the bag out for Hiram. "Winner, winner," he said. "Fish for dinner."

Hiram kept the fish under his coat when he got home. He took his mother's glass Jell-O mold and layered the bottom with pebbles from the garden. He poured cool water into the bowl. Up in his room, he slowly shook the fish into their new home. He set the fishbowl on the carpet. Hiram lay on his belly and rested his head in his palms. His eyes watched the fish mouth at the water. He watched them swim to the bottom and nibble at the pebbles.

"I'll call you Batman," he told the bigger of the two. He pressed his finger against the bowl. "And you can be Robin, since you're smaller." Late into the night he watched Batman and Robin flap and dart. He watched them kiss the water's surface. He'd never seen anything so beautiful. He could hardly believe they were his.

On his way home from school, Hiram used his allowance to buy fish flakes. He held the tube of fish food in his hand like a sprinter's baton. He ran the length of sidewalk to his house. He was eager to feed the duo. As soon as he passed the threshold of his home, his father called him into the bathroom.

"Look what you did," he said. "Look at your mama's Jell-O mold." He pointed to the fishbowl on the counter. "Look at the mess you made."

Hiram kept his eyes on the clean linoleum floor.

"See what happens when we have pets?"

Hiram nodded.

His father lifted the toilet seat. "Go on."

Hiram didn't move. He scratched at his shin with the toe of his sneaker.

His father took a knee in front of Hiram. He took the boy by the chin and forced him to look him in the face. "I am your father," he said. His anger kept his mouth tight as he spoke. "And you know my mind. Go on." He shook the boy's face as he let go of his chin.

Hiram cupped his hand in the fishbowl. He waited for Batman and Robin to eddy into his palm before he ladled them out of the bowl. As gentle as he did at the fair, he brought his fish to the toilet bowl. He poured them from his hands. Their tails flapped, as if shocked by the coolness of the porcelain. They swam the circumference of the bowl.

"Rules are rules," his father said.

Hiram swallowed. He watched the fish peck at the surface.

"Go on. Come ahead now."

Hiram could feel the unopened fish food in his back pocket. He just wanted to feed them, to see them dance around collecting the flakes. The thought of it made his chin shake.

"Get on with it."

Hiram did not look away. As the water flushed he watched them fight against the current. He watched as their sparkled bodies swirled into darkness.

A Taste of Meat

Tutu raked his beak through the plate of lettuce. He chirped and shook his head. Lettuce flung across the counter. He rained salad to the floor.

"I don't think he likes it," the cook said. "I got seeds in the pantry."

"No," Hiram said. "Bird's going to learn to keep clean. He'll eat every scrap he gets." Hiram went to Tutu. He took a pen from his breast pocket and forced the bird's mouth open. "Eat." He shoved a pinch of lettuce into the beak.

Tutu screeched and flapped his wings. His tongue fought against the pen. Lettuce flew from the plate. Hiram packed the beak with more. "I said eat it."

As he put his fingers in the bird's mouth his pen slipped. Taking advantage of the momentary freedom, Tutu clamped down on Hiram's pinkie. His beak snapped through the skin like teeth through a cooked sausage. He clawed at Hiram's hand and vised his beak down to the bone. Hiram tugged his hand free. The tip of his finger dangled from the knuckle. Tutu jumped to the floor. He scuttled to the corner and rolled onto his back, claws out. Beak open and ready to fight. As Hiram's scream melted with the shouts and animal roar of the cafeteria hall, Tutu shook with fear.

*Interview with Dr. Preston Beamon,
Animal Psychologist*

Q. Now, in your own words, why are you here?

A. ---

Q. You understand you're safe here, Tutu. You can open up to me. Feel free to explore, to express yourself. Now, with those ground rules, tell me, what did you do?

A. ---

Q. Alright, I see. Right. You haven't done anything, so you have nothing to say. Now we're getting somewhere. You feel innocent. I get that. Then how has this experience changed you? How has your incarceration shaped you as a bird?

A. ---

Q. Hmmm. I understand it's a tough question. It requires us to look inside ourselves. And that can be a scary place. Hey, it's still scary for me to explore my inner space. Some frightening things in there. Perhaps there's a mother who wouldn't give us approval? A father who wasn't there? Did an uncle touch us in a bad way? I've heard it all, Tutu. I'm not here to judge you. I'm here to help you . . . discover you. Okay?

A. ---

Q. So what I want you to do is close your eyes. Go on. Close them. Picture yourself at a park, or at the beach— really any place you like—somewhere outside these walls. Can you picture it? Do you have your place?

A. ---

Q. Now, in the surrounding comfort of that place, wherever that may be, I want you to look down inside yourself. Go on and get in there. I'll give you a moment. Got it?

A. ---

Q. Now tell me what's down there. Don't be afraid, Tutu. What do you see?

A. ---

Q. Tutu. I'm a patient man. You can sit there and blink at me all you want. But I am going to reach you. You understand that, right?

A. ---

Q. You can be a tough guy. That's fine. But you must realize that without an answer, I have to notate that you're unwilling to cooperate. "Inmate was unresponsive when questioned. Inmate showed no outward signs of remorse." Is that fair, accurate?

A. ---

Q. Look, I've been more than clear that I'm a friend here. So I'm picking up my pen and asking you one last time. What have you learned from your experience here?

A. ---

Q. Have it your way. I'm taking note of this . . . Alright, let's move on. I'm not saying this was a failure, just an area for us to improve. It's an area of opportunity, okay?

A. ---

Q. Fine, look, let's try an exercise. Just a second, let me grab my briefcase . . . Now, this appears to be an orange. It is round, orange in color. When you smell it . . . it smells citrusy. By all empirical measures this is an orange. Heck, I pulled it out of my lunch bag, right?

A. ---

Q. But in all seriousness, Tutu, this is not an orange. Let's imagine this is your anger. Everybody, myself included, has some amount of hate inside. And our hate and anger has a source. It can be from something we don't understand or something we fear. Sometimes it's passed down from our parents. So what I want you to do is take all your anger and pull it from yourself. Release all your hatred and put it into this orange. Here, I'll put the orange in front of you so you can project onto it. Take time to channel your anger into the object . . . Have you emptied yourself?

A. ---

Q. I'll take that as a yes. Now, what do you want to say to your anger?

A. ---

Q. Tutu, please. Will you please not peck at the orange?

A. ---

Q. Come on, Tutu. I want you to speak to your anger. Hey, come on. We're not supposed to eat our anger. You're getting juice everywhere. We don't want to put the hate back inside you. Understand?

A. ---

Q. Hey, stop that. I said quit it. Stop biting the anger. Give me back my orange.

A. ---

Q. Christ. He bit me. Goddamn bird just—son of a bitch bit me. Carl? Can you restrain him? Shit. I'm bleeding. Hey, I'm bleeding here, man. Can we get something—now?

A. ---

Big Bird on the Block

Two inmates sat in the yard smoking menthols down to the filters.

"The fuck is up with that bird?" the first one said.

"Who, Lil' Rich? He's cool."

"No, the bird. That actual bird." He pointed his cigarette at the base of the concrete wall. Tutu huddled there, plucking his feathers. He shook his head and combed his beak through the dirt.

"Man, you don't know Big Bird?"

"That his real name?"

"Hell if I know? Nobody knows his name. I've been here a nickel, ain't heard him say a word." The second inmate ashed his cigarette downwind. "We call him Big Bird, on account that's one bird you don't fuck with."

"For real?"

"Man, you too new to be this stupid. I heard that little birdie straight killed a man. Made one guard transfer out." He held up his hand and pulled on his pinkie. "Popped it right off."

"For real?"

"Already burned through three psychologists. Won't even see him anymore. Can't crack that nut."

They watched the parrot rake through the dirt. Tutu held a jagged rock in his beak. He touched the rock's surface with his tongue. When he realized it wasn't a seed, he shook his head and picked up another pebble.

"What you think he's doing?" the first inmate said.

The second inmate drew from his cigarette. "Probably figuring who to fuck with next." He exhaled through his nostrils. "All I know, you see Big Bird come around, you better act right."

Tutu hopped to a sunny patch of dirt. He closed his eyes and absorbed the heat. His feathers rippled in the wind. A guard wearing leather gloves approached. As the guard came near he slowed and took on a cautious demeanor. He looked ready to wrangle a python.

"What's all that noise?" the first inmate said.

The second inmate laughed. "Maybe he got a visitor."

Tutu sensed the guard's footsteps. He stretched his wings to their limit and the guard recoiled.

"Look at that fool," the second inmate said. "Scared as shit."

The first inmate shook his head. "Why don't he fly away? Man, I had his wings, I'd be gone."

As the guard reached toward Tutu again, Tutu gracefully perched himself on the outstretched glove. There was a reverence in the way the guard held the bird. He carried him like he was the Ark, as if the bird contained some unknown power. For a brief moment the yard fell silent. The men racked their weights and ceased their games. They all watched as the guard carried him like a standard. The second inmate felt small in the presence of such a grand thing. He rubbed the side of his face. "Even if they weren't clipped," he said, "where would he go?"

800 Words or Less

The prison guard removed the receiver from its cradle and placed it in front of Tutu. "Three minutes," the guard said. "I'm to inform you this conversation is monitored." He left the bird to speak with his visitor.

On the other side of the glass was a peculiar looking man. Tutu stretched to look him over. Although he appeared youthful, the man's hair was thinning. Beneath two strange, longing eyes hung dark bags of skin. The visitor hugged the phone between his shoulder and ear. With his good hand he hoisted his left arm onto the ledge. It rested there motionless.

Tutu angled his head to the side. His eyes glossed with memory. "Christoph."

"Hello, Tutu. Been a long time."

Seeing his friend so old and unfamiliar put Tutu at a loss for words.

"Look at you. You look good." Christoph tried to smile but only his cheeks moved. "I'm not sure why I waited so long. I guess I knew I wouldn't have anything good to say."

Tutu leaned low toward the glass. He wanted to tell Christoph that he still remembered the good times. He wanted to talk about the promenade and the clean air. But he knew there wasn't time for sentiment. Christoph wasn't here for that.

"So . . ." Christoph cleared his throat. "Mom died."

"Oh, Christoph." Tutu thought of the first time he saw her from behind the bars of his birdcage, in the back of that cluttered pet store. He remembered her kindness. And the kindness Christoph first showed him. Tutu clicked his tongue.

Christoph's face screwed to the side. "I've been a terrible friend." He began to cry. "That should be me in there."

Tutu tilted his head.

"I could have said something but I didn't. You asked for my help but I just sat there."

"Christoph." Tutu lowered his head.

"No, listen." Christoph smeared tears across his cheek. "I can make it up to you. What if I could get you out of here? You could come live with me. And I could take you back to the park, like we used to. I still have your old cage in the garage."

Tutu shook his head. "No, Christoph."

Christoph placed the phone on his other ear. He searched Tutu's face, trying to understand the bird. But he could not. So his face slid into an expression of deep sadness.

It was a look Tutu knew. It reminded him of the ferrets and the mice of the pet store, the beasts in their cages. And it reminded him of the animals he lived with now. All those sad faces dreaming of flight.

"Sorry," Tutu said. He waddled closer and cocked his head toward his old friend. "Sorry, sorry, sorry."

Behind him the guard unlocked the door. It groaned against the hinges as he entered to take the bird away.

"Wait, Tutu?" Christoph yelled into the phone but there was no reply. He wrapped on the glass and called to him again but there was nothing. The line had gone silent.

DIARY OF A BAD AFTERNOON

On the origins of first love
Every artist needs a mentor, a body of work to plunder until
they're ready to go out and create on their own. It is essen-
tial that we have an influence. I don't know who said that,
but it certainly seems too commonplace to be uniquely my
idea. Either way, on the evening of my seventeenth birthday,
I found myself looking down at my candles wondering what
to wish for. "More than anything," I wished, "I want to be
a writer. A real writer."

But after I blew out the lights and listened to my mother's
exuberant clapping, I knew I didn't have a prayer. I didn't
have anybody to look up to.

I first knew the afternoon before the big dinner. We were
at the department store shopping for shirts. I watched
how he spidered his fingers over the hangers. The way he
left the back of his hand on his waist, elbow cocked like
a fencer. It all started to add up. My son was queer.

"Mom, what about this one?" He held the sleeve up
to his face. "Goes with my skin tone, right?"

I gave him an absent stare.

I could accept a gay son. Perhaps even more. I liked
the idea of getting pedicures together. Or maybe he would
date a man who could show me how to create a focal point
in the living room. How to pillow our sofa. I would like
that. And somehow, I believed in my heart, telling my
book club that my boy was gay would lend me a new cred-
ibility. If I wanted, I could hold fast to a viewpoint that

they couldn't possibly understand without having a gay child of their own.

"Try it on," I told him. "Let's see how it fits."

First time I saw her was in the dressing room. I waited with a shirt in my hand. This was the most important day of my life, and I had this heavy feeling that my mom was going to ruin it. I was drumming my hand on the table-top, when a stunning woman walked behind the counter. Stunning because she wore a combination of clothes I never thought possible. Brown tights, stunning in their tightness. A sheer tunic, stunning in its graceful draping. "Just one?" She wore a headband that would have looked odd on anyone else. But on her, she was transformed into a bohemian beauty. "You have more?"

"No," I said. "Just this." I gave her the shirt.

I'm embarrassed to admit, but J. M. Coetzee became my fa-vorite writer purely by chance. At seventeen and one day old, I went straight to the downtown library. With the help of the reference desk clerk I found a book that listed every writer that ever won The Nobel Prize in Literature. From Sully Prudhomme to Herta Müller, I took in the (mostly) updated list, along with the (mostly) complete bibliography associated with the recipients. It was incredible. It was humbling. Not because of what these names meant to the field of literature— the flame of innovation they had inherited, fed, and passed along brighter—while I was still searching for that spark to ignite my writing. No. It was crushing because out of the hundred names on the list I only recognized a few. Of the names I did know, I'd only read one book (sophomore year

Ms. Sweeney assigned Of Mice and Men *for extra credit).*
Give it to chance, I thought. I took my mother's birth year,
1969. Samuel Beckett would be my new favorite writer. As
the book stated, for his work where the "destitution of mod-
ern man acquires its elevation," he would be my mentor.

In the beginning I attributed Ellis' shy demeanor to him
being a bookish boy. Small boned. He never ran in the
sprinklers with the other kids. Never collected bugs in a
kill jar or broke glass bottles under the streetlights. But
as a young man, a softness remains. There's something he
didn't outgrow. He's not strong and rigid like most men.
In that he's lacking.

To me, a straight man demands. He takes what he
wants. But my boy said things like, "It's okay Mom, order the pizza with olives. I can pick them off." Not only
that, his wrists often dangled. God, on the treadmill—
those limp little hands. Dainty and useless, like a T-Rex.

Through the slatted door, she tells me her name is Marion. I had never met a Marion before.

"I'm going to check on another customer. Let me know
if you need a different size."

I wanted to start a conversation with her, but I didn't
know how. Besides, I figured this was the wrong place for
that anyway. I pressed my ear against the door and listened to her walk down the hall.

When I came out of my booth, Marion was waiting
for me by the mirrors. She leaned both shoulder blades
against the wall, her arms slinking at her sides.

"Looks good on you," she said.

I liked the coolness in her voice.

"The cut is amazing."

After two books I felt destitute. I needed to find a new mentor.

Ellis strode out of the dressing room. His mouth choked a smile and his eyes were airy. "Be honest." He turned to the side and ironed his palm down the placket. "I love the cut."

What kind of man says "cut"?

I shifted my weight and examined the shirt. A pale blue oxford with yellowed buttons. Too bland for the new Ellis. I turned him around and flattened the fabric across his back. His shoulders were angular and biting. He had the body of a gazelle. "I think we can do better. We want to make an impression, right?"

I'd told Mom it wasn't necessary, shopping and all. I was fine with a simple, casual dinner. In fact, I told her that Coetzee would most likely prefer it. He was an ascetic after all. But she insisted that was all the more reason we should flair it up. *Flair it up.* Her words, not mine. I tried to tell her that ascetic had nothing to do with art and beauty, but Mom wouldn't have it. She wanted gusto.

Marion was right. I looked good in this shirt. With her, I felt a confidence I normally couldn't carry.

How those words resonated in me. I knew she was paid to say things like that, but I could tell she meant it. That bored look Marion wore served only as a disguise. She took pride in being earnest. And like me, I think she was an artist at heart. She liked transforming things.

In this shirt I felt like I could talk to her. With a little flair, I knew I would survive the night.

Maybe Mom was on to something.

In a random stroke of luck (maybe that's how love works if you put yourself out there) an essay I was reading about Beckett happened to be penned by J. M. Coetzee. It was a name I recognized from the Nobel list. I went back to my librarian again and asked her, "What's good by Coetzee?" For some reason she gave me a slight grin.

"Excellent choice." She disappeared down the stacks. When she returned, she had two books cradled across her stomach. "If I was you, I'd try these on."

"Take this one. And try this." I handed Ellis bright, beautiful shirts. "This too while you're in there." Ellis made a face like I was pulling out his toenails. So dramatic, my son. I rolled my watch on my wrist. "We've got plenty of time. The dinner's not going to start without you. You have to change out of that anyway." Ellis left for the dressing room. I walked to another rack. My fingers dragged across the length of the fabric. If my son was to be a writer, he would be a well dressed one. And if he was going to be gay, by god he was going to be the sharpest gay man he could be. He would impress that old Coetzee. I would be sure of it. One look at my boy and Coetzee would think, Now there's a talent to look out for.

I decided that today, my son would embrace his own kind of manhood.

"Ellis, wait." I walked to the dressing room. I caught him talking to the shop girl, probably about the cut of his clothes. I gave him the dress shirt. "This pattern is gorgeous," I said. I could tell the shop girl liked it.

He looked at the price tag and his eyes went huge. "Mom, I can't." He quickly handed back the shirt like he was passing off a crying infant.

"It's a special night." I nudged his ribs as he turned toward the dressing room.

I glanced at the shop girl's name tag. "Marion," I said, like I knew her name, "don't let him leave until he's tried on that shirt. Promise me."

She brought her hand next to her face. She crossed her fingers and gave me a smile. It was a shallow thought, but she seemed like a girl a straight Ellis might like.

Marion took the clothes. She counted the hangers and pulled a card with the corresponding number. "Hot date tonight?"

"Not even. I'm having dinner with a writer."

"You a writer?"

I wasn't sure how to answer. "I like to write."

"Who are you meeting?"

My throat cleared. I tried to sound casual. "J. M. Coetzee."

"Never heard of him." Marion took a shirt out of the pile. She let her lips pucker. "Executive decision. You don't want to wear this."

I tilted my head toward a rack of rejects. It was a move I had seen in movies, when a guy wanted another round from a bartender. Marion's flat smile told me it was a move that didn't suit me either.

"Tell me about Coetzee." She took another shirt from the pile and hung it on the rack. "Wow. That's just, wrong."

"Well, he won the Nobel in 2003. He teaches now, in Australia."

"He's flying out here to have dinner with you?" She caught herself. "I mean, no offense."

"It's bizarre, I know. I've never met the man. But I took third place in a writing contest and won dinner with him."

"So you're on your way. Mr. Bigshot writer." Marion set the clothes on the counter.

"I don't know about that. It's a bronze medal, wasn't even that good."

"Dinner with Coetzee." Her ripe brown eyes got big, like she was ready to die a good death. "Ellis, that's amazing."

I looked at the floor. I felt desire aching in me. She forced me to feel it, deep in my body.

"Next time someone asks, say you're a writer." She hooked the shirts on her hand and began to walk me to a room. She stopped in the hall, her face was twisted in thought. "If you get a night with a Nobel laureate, what'd first prize get, a golden typewriter?"

"Something like that. Coffee with Franzen."

"I've heard of him."

Mom came into the dressing room with another shirt. "Ellis," she said. "Isn't this a delicious pattern?"

I had never heard my mom use *delicious* like that before. And I wasn't sure why she was using it now. Marion eyed the garment. She looked like she might gag.

It was love at first line. I couldn't put my finger on it, but there was something sublime about the first line of Disgrace. *I didn't know why, but there was something perfect in his words. "For a man of his age, 52, divorced, he has, to his mind, solved the problem of sex rather well." It seemed serious enough. The poor guy was aging and alone. He had lost something. But there was a soft chord of humor ringing in there. Tender, but dark. One line in, and I knew Coetzee was the one for me.*

A month ago the mail had come and Ellis started yelling in the kitchen. "Cozy, cozy," he screamed. I hurtled through the living room, expecting to find him cut and bleeding. But he was doubled over by the island, a letter in his fist.

"Are you hurt? Can you make it to the car?"

He raised up and grabbed the counter like it would save him. "They picked me. I can't believe I won."

I pointed to the letter. "You won what?"

"I got third."

"Honey, that's great. Why didn't you tell me you were playing sports?"

Ellis flattened the letter on the butcher block. "An essay thing. 1,000-word competition. Second runner-up gets to have their favorite writer come to their house for dinner. They picked me."

"You won a free dinner?"

"Coetzee. He's coming here, for dinner."

"Who?"

Ellis pulled a book from the shelf. He showed me Cozy's picture on the dust jacket. The man looked like an extinct bird. His skin was pallid and cracked. His mouth sliced to the side and one shoulder sloped, locking him in a frail, crooked pose. I turned it over and read the cover. "Diary of a Bad Year." Try, *Diary of a Bad Decade.* "That's great, Ellis."

This can't be him, I thought. This is the man my son adores?

I looked hideous. My reflection spoke to it. The shirt was so bright it felt humid. Tangerine and purple, creamsicle and violet, swirled into a nightmare sunset. Expensive buttons—*exorbitant* might be the right word—dotted down the shirt. The collar was thick as a slice of pie. And the inside of the cuffs contrasted with the outside pattern of the shirt.

"Ellis. Ellis, come out. Let's see it." My mother was waiting out there. But I couldn't let Marion see me like this.

I began to feel that terrible feeling. Sick and embarrassed, like waiting to be picked up from school. Seeing that station wagon tug down the lane. Praying to anything that would listen, Please don't let them see me.

Mom was going to ruin it with Marion. And she would ruin it with Coetzee too. Deep down I knew it.

At the market, I had told her Coetzee was a teetotaler. She still thought it was a kind gesture to offer wine with dinner. I told her Coetzee fulminated against all forms of animal cruelty. He wouldn't dream of eating animals.

Mom told me, "And that's why we're having fish."

"No," I said. "Christ, he's vegetarian. He won't even wear things made from animals."

And now she kept bringing things to Marion, having me try them on. Exotic leather belts made from alligator and ostrich. Calfskin driving moccasins. I knew she meant well, but this wasn't the first time she had done this.

With a renewed exuberance I showed the book to my English teacher. "This is writing if I ever saw it," I told her.

"What do you like about it?" She sat in the desk next to me. "Why does it work for you?"

I stared at the line, thinking of something smart to say,

trying to recall the grammar and vocabulary she'd been pounding into our heads that year. But the words failed me. "It makes me want to read more."

She smiled down at the desk. "What more could you ask?"

Looking at a rack of belts, I wondered which one would best suit my new son. Something braided? Perhaps one that resembled a polished alligator? The buckles flared the light like summer on a windshield. It reminded me of something I had heard in the car the other day. This doctor lady said everything in our children pointed back to genetics and environment. Called it nature and nurture—which I liked. Because I blamed this sudden queerness on his father. It's his fault for never being there. Instead of showing him how to burn a steak on the grill, Ellis had to learn that room-temperature egg whites made stiffer meringue. He learned that cream of tartar helped the peaks hold. When Ellis should have been in the garage poking under the hood, he was in the dining room, trimming the candle wicks.

What was I to do?

I saw an ostrich skin belt with fat dark stitching. The silver toned buckle looked liquid. This one stood out. Now this was the belt for my Ellis. I took it to the shop girl.

In the sixth grade my class took a field trip to a conservation center. We had been studying all month about recycling and the dangers of swelling landfills. The whole class was waiting by the curb with Miss Leighton. It was cold that morning and the bus was late. The boys shivered and tried to pretend like it wasn't that cold, while the girls were smart enough to huddle in packs and stamp their feet. As we waited, my mom pulled to the curb. She'd bought a coffee for Miss Leighton and hot chocolate for the class. She began to pour from a disposable carafe. Mom was filling cup after styrofoam cup, lining them up on the car hood.

The class began to stir. Most of the kids were excited at this vision. But the smarter ones protested. "Litterbug," one kid said. He pointed to the sleeve of cups. "Those aren't biodegradable. Your mom's a litterbug." Other kids joined in the commotion. Some were so conflicted they declined it all together. "Miss Leighton, that's bad," one girl said. "We learned those cups are bad. We can't have them."

My mom laughed. "You know, you're right. I should have thought of that." She put her palm on her forehead and made a face that had my classmates laughing too.

I was mortified. I could feel my chin tremble. The wind kicked up and bit at my eyes. They began to sting and water. By the time the bus arrived, the class rushed to the door. They had already forgotten the whole thing. But I hadn't. The embarrassment gnawed to the middle of my bones. I waited at the end of the line. I pressed my back against the bus and let the engine's idle vibrate through my chest. It shook the tears from my eyes and they jagged down to my chin. I wanted it to stop. But the more I thought about it, the more I cried.

Miss Leighton had me sit next to her in the front seat of the bus. As we rode I stared at myself in the window, wishing I had a different mom. I kept wiping at my cheeks, smearing the tears across my face. Miss Leighton pinched my arm. I looked at her. She was staring straight ahead. I went back to the window and she pinched me again. I could tell she was hiding a smirk. "Don't let them get you," she said. "You have a great mom. I didn't see anybody else do something that thoughtful." Her head swayed as the bus roared through a turn. "You're a lucky kid to have a mom like that."

But now, in the changing room, I couldn't keep stalling. I knew I looked ridiculous. But I shouldn't hold it against her.

The opening of Disgrace *does everything. First, it is clear and concrete. Coetzee's writing is easy to read, using plain but descriptive language. His gambit is also loaded with character information. We learn the age of the protagonist, 52. We are told about his past. He is a divorcé. Coetzee also hints that intercourse has been a problem of sorts for the protagonist. There is mystery and intrigue. What difficulty did this character have with sex? We learn that our main character has a means to cope and correct the conflicts in his life. In short, he has something vital at stake. There is something for him to lose. All in one line!*

I described this to my English teacher (in not so many words) the following day. She seemed impressed enough. But she showed me how I had missed something crucial.

"What's the point of view?" she asked of me. "What about the tense?"

"Third person limited," I said. "That's why I feel so close to the protagonist. Like I'm inside the head of David Lurie."

"Look again," she said. She ran her finger along the first line of the book. "He's writing in present perfect. You realize how rad that is?"

I asked the sales associate what kind of person wears these jeans.

"I'm not sure I understand," he said.

"This pair, here." I held them out. "Who wears these?"

"Men," he said. "They're men's jeans."

"I know that. But what kind of a man?" I let my voice lower. "Are these gay jeans?"

The associate looked at me, cross. "I'm not sure denim has that kind of orientation."

"Well, then what type of person would wear this style?"

The associate tilted his head. He curled a finger under his lips. "They are really tight. I mean tight, tight." His voice croaked at the end of his sentence. "It'd have to be someone ballsy. Lots of confidence."

Confident, ballsy. It takes balls to put yourself out there like my son does. "That gal in the changing room, Maryann, can you take these to her? Ask her to give them to my son. She'll know who he is."

The jeans were so tight they pinched at my balls. I pulled at the crotch and lifted a leg but there was no give. I tried to stretch them out. I yanked at the thighs. I even crouched down into a squat.

Marion wrapped on the door. "Okay in there?"

"I'm not sure."

Marion gave a soft laugh that put me at ease. "If you're wondering, they're supposed to feel tight. It's the style."

"I feel ridiculous."

"Come on, man up," she said. "Come out and show me. I'll wait by the mirrors."

I couldn't help but walk with incredible posture. The jeans forced a tall, confident gait. I stood before the three-way mirror. Marion slid behind me. Her eyes traveled up my body.

"The pants look amazing. But this," she circled her hand at my torso, "is out of control."

I looked at our reflection. In the sides of the three-way mirror the two of us stood together. Over and over, as a couple, we went on forever. I wanted to stay there with her. She wiped at a thread on my shoulder. I watched her ten million hands touch me. My heart went fast and I felt like there wasn't enough blood in my body.

"You pair those jeans with the first shirt you had on. Now we're talking."

"What about this one?"

"Just toss it," she said.

"But my mom loves it."

"Tell her it's a compromise. You wear the jeans she likes and the shirt that we like."

Hearing her say *we* opened a galaxy of possibilities in my brain. She rolled the cuffs of the flamboyant shirt. It made me look like an ice dancer. "Or there's this," she said. "You could get this one too."

"But I hate it. Look at it."

"It gives you an excuse to return it." She looked at my face in the mirror, waited for our eyes to meet. "I wouldn't mind hearing how dinner went."

To use my teacher's term, Coetzee is indeed rad. The second book my librarian recommended, Diary of a Bad Year, *was just as powerful. This time he utilized the first person for both main characters. And again, an old man falls for a young woman. Hopeless in love. Something that struck me more than I expected.* Diary *begins with another simple and arresting line. "My first glimpse of her was in the laundry room."*

A child hid from his mother. He made a fort inside a circular rack of shirts. The child parted the fabric and poked his nose into the light. I watched him scout for his mother. The smell of sugared milk panted from his mouth.

"Brayden," his mother called as she focused on shopping. "Come out, Brayden." Her voice was indifferent. This was a game they'd played before.

Brayden opened the shirts wide and stretched his neck. He was too clumsy to properly hide. When he saw me, I winked. His head darted behind the garments.

His mother went to another rack of clothes, screeching the hangers against the rod. "I'm leaving, Brayden. You better come out."

Brayden poked his head out again. His eyes showed fear.

I looked at the child. "You can hide if you want, but you'll be all alone." My voice softened to a whisper. "I bet your mommy will love you if you come out of there." He held to the sleeve of a shirt and looked for his mother before darting out and clutching her leg.

"Mom," Ellis said from behind. He had a shopping bag in his hand. The shop girl was with him too.

"Where are the clothes? I wanted to see the new you."

"You will," he said.

"You got the belt, and the shoes?"

He looked to the shop girl and he nodded.

"We got him that shirt you liked too," she said.

"You're not worried Cozy will get mad?"

"Coetzee?" Ellis shrugged and gave a frown. "I don't know," he said. "I can't say I know a thing about him."

How could I not read on? The character's yearning to see more of this "her" was my yearning. And perhaps that is what makes Coetzee my favorite writer, whose work I'll plunder until I can go on my own. Like his characters, I find myself hidden in plain view, observing the world and aching to find my place in it. Whether it's family or school, I've always felt a little strange. Hopeless with love, but loving nonetheless. Somehow Coetzee's work makes me feel okay with that. As the Nobel book described him, he is a writer who "portrays the surprising involvement of the outsider."

Encountering Coetzee had made my wish come true.

III
LOVERS

MY ROBERTA

One morning I looked at my wife and caught her staring at our bedroom ceiling. There was something terrible in the way she watched our ceiling fan wobble. Like she was considering all that was wrong with the room and the weight of it wouldn't let her blink.

How long she had been doing that, I didn't know. And I didn't ask because I didn't want to "have a conversation" about it. Instead, I closed my eyes and pretended I was still asleep. I tried to imagine everything was fine. But in the darkness behind my eyelids I could hear her mumbling. It sounded like she was praying. "If this is it," I heard her say, "if this is all there is, Lord Jesus, kill me now."

• • •

My wife, Roberta, I don't even recognize her anymore. Her behavior grows stranger everyday. Just last month she got her clitoris pierced. She didn't tell me or anything. I had to discover it myself. She had just showered and had her foot on the sink. As she was drying off I saw it glinting there between her legs, a metal stud big enough to hang a towel from. Out of nowhere she does this. And where she got the idea, I don't know.

I said to her, "Is there something you'd like to tell me?"

"No," she said.

"How about that," I said. "That thing, hanging from your clitoris there."

"What, this?" She tickled the stud. "This is called the

hood, Curtis, not the clit." And with that, she wrapped the towel around her head. Conversation over.

• • •

A week later—out of the blue—she bought a motorcycle. She went down to the dealership and drained our entire vacation fund. I was out edging the yard when she came rumbling in with this black beast of a thing shaking between her legs. I stopped what I was doing and watched her park it on a sprinkler head. She swung her leg around the gas tank and lumbered into the house.

Twenty years we've been married and she's a stranger to me now.

• • •

One night, coming in from a ride, she said to me, "Curtis, you have no idea." She went to the kitchen table and slouched in a chair.

"Dinner's ready," I said. "There's a plate in the microwave."

Roberta pulled at her bangs. "It takes so much concentration—I'm telling you—it's a miracle I don't lay that bike down. Every time I roll on the throttle I feel it growl against me. It's like a thousand fingertips touching me." She leaned deep into her chair. "All over my body there's this . . . electricity. To the ends of my toenails." She let her mouth twitch like she was savoring the last moment of a secret.

For the third night in a row I warmed her dinner. I sat across the table and watched her exert an amazing effort to eat. She lifted her fork like it was a paint can. After each bite she would exhale loud through her nostrils. Even then, I could tell she was thinking about that motorcycle.

• • •

After that, Roberta started cussing. The Roberta I knew never cussed.

It began at the art walk. Like always, we were at the mall to buy a pretzel and a lemonade, to stroll around and browse the window displays. And we were there for the art fair. Someone at work said there was nothing like seeing a real painting, one on canvas, with brushstrokes pushed into the oil. I'd heard when you dimmed the lights on a painting like that, the landscape would fade. But if the artist painted light in the windows, they would still glow with life inside.

Just beyond the food court was a booth with pastel paintings of oceans and flowers. "Have a look here," I told Roberta. I made her stop and look at a canvas called *Sea-side Cottage*. There was a cottage on an ocean cliff. Moss grew on the roof and a twist of smoke spilled from the chimney. Roberta had a kitchen calendar full of prints like this. Cottages and cabins. Lakes and sea spray. For our anniversary I wanted to buy her a canvas painting. I wanted to hang it over our mantel and install a dimmer switch.

I put my arms around Roberta. "Wouldn't it be nice to have a little home like that? Just the two of us with all that peace and calm."

Roberta leaned toward the painting and squinted. "I don't know."

This caught the artist's attention. He got out of his chair and stood next to us. "You've got a good eye," he said. "This is one of my favorites." He dimmed the light above the painting and like magic, time had passed and the cottage was eased into that good light. But the light in the windows somehow still flickered bright. He stood back and let us take in what he had done.

"That's incredible," I said.

Roberta tilted her head.

"What do you think?" he said.

She made a face like she wanted to spit. "You're joking, right?" She looked dead straight at the man. "What kind of dipshit would want this?"

•   •   •

On the drive home Roberta had the windows down. What her hurry was I didn't know, but she drove reckless. Her head was halfway out the window and she let the car drift out of her lane.

I tried to roll the window but the child-lock was on. "You mind?" I said. "I'm catching a draft here."

Roberta closed her eyes as her hair flapped on her face. "Jesus, Curtis. Live a little."

"Would you watch it?" Up ahead a lady pushed her baby into the crosswalk and Roberta wasn't slowing. I grabbed the dashboard. "Take it easy," I said. "There's people."

Roberta waited for the panic to hit my eyes before she mashed on the brakes. The tires chirped and the nose of the car stopped short of the crosswalk. The mother startled. She glared at us before staring at me like I had something to do with it. Like I was supposed to control the woman next to me. She was leery, moving past the front of our car. As she rolled past, the wind kicked up and spun a diaper from the stroller.

"Jesus," Roberta said. "Look at this."

With one hand on the stroller the mother stretched to collect the diaper, but a gust tumbled it beyond her reach.

"What is this, amateur hour?" Roberta gave a tiny shrug. "Can we go already? Seriously, who does this?"

I dropped in my seat. "Please, Berta. Just let it go."

As the mother stuffed the diaper in her diaper bag Roberta honked. The woman snapped her head to look at us. More startled or appalled I wasn't sure.

"Come on, Roberta. She's got a baby." But before I could do anything, and before the woman had a chance to move, Roberta had her head out the window.

"Move, you fat cunt."

I watched the mother's face burn from a shade of embarrassment to a deeper kind of red. She marched the stroller to my side of the car and Roberta honked the horn again. Twice. Three times she honked at her. She looked at me and laughed as she honked again at the woman.

"Christ, Roberta. The hell is wrong with you?" I tried to roll the window again but Roberta still had it locked.

"Watch out, Curtis. She's a live one."

The mother was at my ear, spittle hurling from her mouth. "Shit, Roberta. Roll it up. Drive already." I shielded my face as the woman began slapping at my head. "Sorry. We're sorry," I said. "Please, Roberta, just go."

Roberta kept laughing. "I don't know, Curtis. She looks fired up. Better do something."

I wanted to scream. I wanted to tell her that Roberta hadn't been herself lately. But I kept finding myself yelling sorry, pleading for her to stop, begging Roberta to drive.

•   •   •

That night I met my friend Perry for beers. I had a hard

time explaining it to him and he didn't seem to believe a word. As I told him about it the edge of his mustache kept pulling toward his ears.

"She kept hitting me until, finally, Roberta drove off," I said.

He glanced over his shoulder. "She called her a cunt?"

"No, Perry. She called her a fat cunt."

His mouth puckered like he'd just swallowed a whiskey.

"It's more than that," I said. "You add in the motorcycle clubs, the late nights, and body piercings. What are you supposed to make of all that?"

Perry tilted his chin to the bartender. He waved two fingers between us. "Bourbon," he said. "Look, I've known Roberta a long time. There's got to be some variable to the problem. Might be a reaction to something."

I didn't like the way he said problem. It made me want to punch him, square in the nose.

"If you had to guess—just throwing it against the wall here—you noticed anything strange?"

The only thing I could think of was a few months back, before I caught her staring. Roberta and I had been making love, same as we always do, but this particular night I got a tickle in my nose. And while I was still on top of her I sneezed one of those toe curling, whole body sneezes. And with me still inside her, my body pitched way in, like never before. Roberta screamed. She called out so sharp I thought for sure I had just done something terrible. I got off her and wiped the hair from her face. "I'm sorry," I said. "You alright? I'm so sorry."

"Yes," Roberta said and with both hands she grabbed me. "Get back here. My God, yes."

A month later she had metal hanging from her lady parts and a hog between her legs.

"Honestly, Perry," I tore at my bar napkin, "I have no idea."

Perry shrugged and raised his bourbon. "Well it's like my daddy always said, If you can't get them filthy rich, might as well get them filthy."

I gave him a look. "Jesus, Perry. That's my wife."

• • •

On Wednesday night I made popcorn. Wednesday we leave all the pillows on the bed so we can sit up and watch *Law & Order*. I brought the popcorn to our room. Roberta had the bed turned down, the pillows strewn on the floor.

"What are you doing?" I said.

In a sad catlike impersonation, she crawled across the bed. She took a DVD from under the mattress. "I want you to do this with me."

"It's Thursday. I made popcorn."

"I want us to do everything they do."

"On *Law & Order*?"

Her voice got low and throaty. A voice that belonged to a cartoon villain, an evil queen. "Just turn it on. Play with me."

So we watched it together. And this is what passed for smut these days: five minutes in, the man with the waxed scrotum had his way with the girl. A young thing with spindly arms and giant breasts. He patty-caked her breasts with his dick. She moaned and twisted her nipples. Then he squeezed her throat until her eyes teared up. Black makeup spilled down her face. He stuck his fingers in her throat. He pried her mouth wide open.

"Do it," Roberta said. "Spit in my mouth." She positioned herself beneath me. She opened her mouth full.

"I can't," I said.

"Just do it," she said. "Pull my head back. Spit in my mouth."

"My mouth is dry."

Roberta pushed her fingers against the back of my tongue. I gagged, and my mouth filled with spit. "Now do it."

The camera was looking down the man's chest now. His point of view. And I was happy to not look at his balls slapping against the girl anymore. But now he was thrusting it in the poor girl's face. He had her on her knees and it looked like her jaw was about to give out. But he ignored her cries and the mascara smearing down her face. He kept pumping at her mouth until her eyes were bugging from her head.

"Here," Roberta said. "Like this. Do it rough." She took my hands and pressed them against her throat.

"What is this?"

"What I want." She tightened her fingers on mine. "Keep going. Just like that. Tighter. Don't stop."

I freed my hands and put them on her breasts. But she grabbed me again and made me choke her. "Tighter," she said. Her mouth fell open and I could hear the air struggle to get in. Her forehead filled with blood. "There it is." She clasped my wrists. My hands went tighter, deeper into her throat until I felt her pulse throb. Then I felt a different thing. The metal stud quivering between her legs, and I felt her come like never before. Her whole body was shuddering uncontrollably.

When we finished she collapsed on the bed.

I went to brush the hair from her eyes but she knocked my hand away.

"Don't touch me. Not now."

"Let me get a towel."

"Leave it," she said. "We don't have to clean up yet. Just leave it alone." She twisted herself in the sheets. I stared at the ceiling and listened to her sleep. The ceiling fan creaked. It looked like it might spin off the ceiling, any day now, and come crashing down on us. I thought about how I might fix it.

•   •   •

In our backyard, next to the grill, Roberta sat in a lawn chair. It was the kind of day when it was good to be outside so she rolled her sleeves to her shoulders. I handed her a bottle from the ice chest.

"Happy anniversary," I said.

"This is fucking nice." She leaned her face back to take in more light. She curled her toes into the lawn. "We should move, you know. Just pack a bag and leave it all." Her voice sounded drugged.

"Where?" I said. "What about the house?" But she didn't answer. She had just come back from another ride and was spent.

As she slept in the sun, I went inside to get the meat. On the refrigerator I saw a picture of us from decades ago, our honeymoon. There were palm trees behind us and past that was an ocean. Neither of us looked at the camera. We both looked at something just out of view. And for whatever reason we smiled at what we saw. Roberta with her hair, feathered and wavy, framing the length of her face. Roberta with tinted lenses the size of orange slices. That quiet, mousy Roberta, faded and grainy, held in my arms. And there I was. My stupid shaggy hair. Me and my high school mustache that would never fill in all the way. I'm right behind her, holding my girl tight like my life depended on it. I believed we were happy then. And I wondered if we could go back. If I could get her to sell that bike, even at a loss, would we have enough to get us back there? To take another picture with her in my arms.

I set the meat next to the grill. I brought out the buns, too, so I could toast them the way she liked. While I waited for the charcoal to ash over, Roberta slept. The sun was hanging low now, and it cast that magic light on our home. The smooth light made it seem like a sad thing. The sprinkler head, busted and weeping, in the corner of the yard. The gutter sagging from the edge of the roof. How could she sleep so peacefully while everything around her was falling apart? As I watched her chest rise and fall I wanted nothing more than to wake her with the feeling of my hands coming down tight on her throat. What I'd give to hold her there until the lights went out.

Instead, I slapped the hamburger into patties and threw them on the fire. I watched the smoke swirl around Roberta. Her drink had begun sweating in the sun and was slipping from her fingers. It tilted from her hand. The bottle threatened to tumble on the ground, to shatter and make a mess of things, but I didn't move. I let it stay as it was.

BLOCKBUSTER

I had made up my mind to leave Doug. It's these Thursdays. They're killing me.

Thursday is date night. Every Thursday we go to Outback Steakhouse and start with one of those fried onions. First course, Doug tells me how they have the best croutons here. Then he asks our waiter what all the different sauces are and what's in them and still orders the sirloin. I complain when my salmon comes out dry. After we share the molten cake it's off to the video store. Then we go home for popcorn and as the credits start to roll I wait for Doug to make his move, pressing down on my shoulders, holding his breath with the hope I'll give him a blowjob.

The only variety on date night is the movie. Being civil adults and all, we have joint custody of who gets to pick. On my weeks, I'll spice it up with a foreign film, or something classic that won a bunch of awards. But this is Doug's week, which means we're getting something stupid.

I went my own way at the video store. I didn't care to be around Doug as he was picking out his movie, so I browsed the romantic comedy section. All the titles had covers with women frozen in silly poses. A lady leaning over and laughing so hard all her teeth were showing. Or another with a couple holding each other, but the girl is pulling away and making this face right at the audience, telling us she has commitment issues. There were rows of them. All those faked emotions, everything painfully staged.

"Think I got a winner," Doug said. He came up behind me, tapping a video case in his hand.

"Let me guess. There's a situation and some agent comes out of retirement for one last job."

He looked at the back of the video. "Nope."

"Is there *Justice* or *Executive* in the title?"

He showed me the cover. A man held a pistol next to his face and squinted at some unseen danger. *Marked for Vengeance.*

"Great," I said.

"You might like it. See, he's a DEA agent and his partner gets murdered. But the twist is, his partner was a K-9 dog."

"Can a dog get murdered? Isn't murder reserved for people?"

Doug shook his head. "He's an officer of the law. People get life for that."

As we waited to pay, I thought about those dumb pictures on the movie boxes. It reminded me of when Doug and I got engaged. We had to take engagement photos and the photographer told us we should go to the woods. He took us to a place where the trees fell away and there was a clearing. We stood there and laughed and kissed. All the while the photographer snapped away with his camera. The whole time all I could think was, why I am in the forest wearing my best party dress? And who in their right mind would stand in a field making these stupid faces? The photographer kept shouting at us, "Yes. Yes." Then he'd adjust my posture. "More of that," he said. "What a perfect looking couple," he said, when he didn't know a thing about us. The whole time we were out there the brush was scratching my legs to hell. But I had grinned through it all.

"This is going to be a bad film," I said.

"Like you know."

"This won't end well."

"It's a movie," Doug said. "You don't have to get all uppity."

"We're watching it together."

"I sit through your week too, you know. That black and white bullshit. That foreign shit." Doug set his jaw. "You think I want to read subtitles while I'm trying to watch a movie?"

I thought of a thousand things I had done for him and hated. It made me mad enough to spit on him. But we were in public and I wasn't sure who was watching. So I gave the store an easy smile.

On the way to our car I saw a mix of teenagers hanging their legs off the edge of a truck bed. One of the boys passed a bottle to a girl. She leaned away but he pushed it on her anyway. As she tilted the bottle, the group cheered and the boy slid his arm under her breasts and around her ribs. He ensnared her and licked at her ear. Liquor spilled down her chin. She gagged a little but kept at it. For her effort they cheered even more.

I wanted to warn that girl. I wanted to tell her she couldn't take back what they were going to do to her. But I felt Doug pulling my arm, steering me clear of them.

Most of the way home we didn't speak. We listened to the radio until I couldn't take the noise any longer. I turned it off.

"I like that song," Doug said. He turned it back on.

I cranked the volume down. "Why'd you pull me to the car like that?"

"What?" He forced a playful laugh.

"I'm serious."

"They're just kids, Lauren. It's not like we're their parents."

"I feel sorry for their parents. That poor girl."

"It's the summer. They're having fun. We used to do the same thing." Doug looked at me and I couldn't tell if he winked or if the muscle twitch in his cheek was acting up again. "Remember that? Those hot summers." He put his hand on my thigh and squeezed.

It seemed as good a time as any to tell him I was leaving him. But I wasn't sure how to start. And I didn't want things getting heated while I was trapped in the car. I turned the volume up on the radio. The rearview mirror shook and distorted the road. That girl, that howling pack of boys, must have been gone by now. I wondered where they'd take her.

After the movie was over, and after Doug was finished and sleeping, I stole out the front for a cigarette. I went down past the steps to the flower bed, so I wouldn't get ash on the porch. It was late and the heat still hung in the air. I could smell Doug on my skin. And my fingers trembled as I smoked.

Down the sidewalk, I saw my neighbor coming in from a walk with his little dog. The dog pulled at the leash, but my neighbor kept him reined in. When the leash snagged at his collar the dog shuddered and pulled a tight circle before trying to run ahead. "Easy," he kept telling the dog as he tugged the leash.

I waved as he passed the edge of our yard.

"Ms. Lauren." He stopped and rested his foot on our steps. "Didn't see you at the homeowners meeting."

"Miss anything good?"

He grazed his hand along our bush. "Shrubs no higher than thirty-six inches. Smoking is now designated to back porches only."

"Really." I ashed my cigarette. "You going to tell on me?"

"We didn't see anything," he said to his dog. "Did we?" He picked him up and let him lick his face.

A man and his dog. It seemed like a good thing. And I wanted to know how he came about such a good thing. "Are you happy?" I said.

"Sorry?"

"You and Marvin." I tilted my head toward their house. "You guys seem to have it together."

He closed both eyes and flattened his mouth. "Child, please," he said. "We keep appearances, but we keep better fences." The dog tried to jump from his arms, but my neighbor held him tight. "How's Douglas these days?"

"Same," I said. I watched the dog shiver in the heat. It looked at me with wide, nervous eyes. "You ever let him off the leash?"

"Out back we do. But he'd dart off out here."

"My whole life I've had one dog."

"Didn't think you and Douglas were dog people."

"When I was a kid. Her name was Pepper."

"Pepper." He stroked between the dog's eyes. "How cute."

"She was half German shepherd, half something else. But she was a good dog. Knew tricks and everything."

"That's great." He kept petting his dog as he looked past me, trying to see into our house.

"Back then we lived next to a pasture. And if we didn't tie her up, Pepper would run off our property, jet out to the neighbor's field. So one day she's out there, off the leash and running, and her paw gets snapped in one of those fox traps."

My neighbor made a sour face. "Oh, no," he said. He shifted the dog to his other arm. "Poor thing."

"Know what a dog does when it's stuck like that?"

The dog was licking his master's knuckle now. My neighbor shook his head.

"You'll love this." I twisted my cigarette into the flower bed. "Somehow a dog knows when it's hopeless. So she gnawed it off. Beneath the knee, right through the bone. And she still had the sense to limp all the way back home."

He stopped petting his dog and gave me a feeble smile. He looked concerned. Just not enough to ask.

"We had to put her down after that," I said. "Don't know why my father insisted on shooting her. She'd have been fine on three legs. Wouldn't have had to tie her up anymore. But he put her down anyway. Said it was the right thing to do with a lame dog."

My neighbor's mouth fell slightly ajar. As his focus shifted from my house to his, the dog leapt from his arms, blasting for the street. For a moment I thought the dog just might break free. A surge to the road and no looking back. Those ratty little claws clicking away on the asphalt, past the last light post, and gone, faded and free into an unknown darkness. But my neighbor yanked the leash tight and kept the thing near. "Come on, boy," he said. "We'd better get inside. Daddy's waiting."

ROUGH AIR

Back when you could carry liquids on an airplane, a woman got me drunk. I was flying to Los Angeles to take Lauren out to dinner. It was about time to ask her to marry me. But thinking about it caused a panic in my head like I was drowning.

From the aisle seat I watched each face board the plane. My hope was to sit next to a foreigner or a businessman. We could both nod and acknowledge our coexistence, then spend the next two hours ignoring each other. I wanted some peace. I wanted to figure things out before I landed.

A fat man stopped at my row. He dragged a carry-on the size of a love seat. It upset me that he was carrying so much onto a plane this small. His oversized body. And his oversized bag that somebody should have seized before he got on. He went to work jamming the dumb bag in the overhead bin, puffing air out his nostrils the whole time. He sounded like he'd pedaled here on a bike. Listening to him breathe, right over my head, made me angry. When he had finished with his luggage, he studied his ticket. His eyes tightened behind his glasses. "Fifteen," he said. "Section D. I think you're in my seat. I have the aisle."

"Thirteen," I said. "Fifteen is back there."

He scratched his scalp and counted down the rows.

"Here, sir." I tapped the ceiling next to the sign. It clearly said 13D. "You're two rows back." But he wouldn't move. It was like he didn't believe me, that for whatever reason me and the signs in front of him had conspired against him. So he kept blimping over me until I was ready to move just to get away from him.

"Come on," a lady said. "There's enough seats." She stood behind him in the aisle. She had sharp features that made her seem angrier than she probably was. But I liked the way she handled the man. "Just take the next one. We're not going anywhere until you sit down." She pressed herself against him and he was urged to leave. She'd had her way with him.

"Sorry about that," she said. She glanced at her ticket. "Looks like I've got the window."

I unbuckled my safety belt.

"Don't. I can manage." She side stepped in front of me, straddling my knees. As her legs spread, her dress cinched drum-tight against her body. I leaned back as far as I could and tried not to notice. But she had a gravity I couldn't ignore.

She took her seat and I watched how her body moved. Everything about her was compact. She was small and smooth like a bird of prey. Her nose hooked from her skull and her cheeks were too wide for her face. She held an odd kind of attraction which made me uneasy sitting so close to her. I leaned away from her until my lap-belt cut at my thighs.

I told myself Lauren was a good woman. She was perfect for me. Stable and patient. She was reasonable—more than that. Lauren was a saint. I had a good woman waiting for me. I volleyed this thought in my head. But the woman beside me had a wildness about her that tore at my best intentions. She knew she looked good. It showed in the way she pulled her hair back fast and clean. Or the way her hand swam through the air to turn on the overhead light. She was dipped in confidence.

Pretending to read, I thumbed through a magazine. I watched her unsaddle her purse. It was an expensive bag.

That much I could tell. Lauren had one like it that she housed in a felt box in her closet. Before we could go out, she would take it out and buff the bag. Lauren hardly put anything in that big bag, but she gleamed when she had it on her shoulder. This woman kicked her purse beneath the seat. She tossed it around like a disposable luxury. As I perused an ad for the best orthopedic surgeons in California I made up my mind to ignore this woman. I knew Lauren wouldn't have it. And I knew what I was capable of doing. But most of all, I knew there was a beautiful danger in the way she drew one leg against the other. No, I would not talk to her.

"Can we just get this over with?" she said.

"Pardon?"

"Come on, really." She extended her hand. I did not take it, but she nudged it closer. Her wrist was sturdy for a girl her size. "Veronica. I'm in HR. Girl's weekend with a college roommate." The strength of her grip surprised me. I released my hand from hers.

"I'm Doug. Police Department. I'm going to see my girlfriend."

"Isn't that fun." She uncapped a tube of lip gloss and ran it around her mouth.

"I'm going to propose."

Veronica let her mouth tug to the side. "Terrible idea."

"Excuse me?"

"Cops aren't any good at marriage. But I'm sure you know this already." She reached overhead and pressed the call button.

I tried to ignore it, but her comment made me itch. "What do you mean?"

"Is this working?" She leaned over me to examine the button. "Did you hear it ding? I don't think this works."

Veronica jabbed the button. I could feel her breasts jostle the air by my face. I shifted toward the aisle.

"What do you mean 'terrible'? How is that terrible? You don't even know me."

"It's not just cops. Nobody's good at it really. Half my job is updating paperwork. Such a hassle changing last names."

There was something about her I couldn't grasp. The way she poached my attention. She made me feel like I was being handled. I wanted her to think I was bored with the conversation. I flipped to another page in the magazine as loud as I could. "Veronica, it was a pleasure. But I have to get some reading done." I focused on the page, a map near the back with arcing blue lines showing all the non-stop flights you could take. From the corner of my eye, I thought I saw her smirk.

The flight attendant tapped our call button. The cut of her blazer made her seem impossibly tall.

"I'd like to place an order," Veronica said.

"This button is reserved for emergencies." The attendant spoke to Veronica with that odd blend of nonsense and graciousness. "Like a heart attack or the need for immediate medical attention."

"Great. We need two cups of ice," Veronica said. "It's an emergency. Overflowing with ice. And an unopened can of tonic." The attendant feigned an apology. She tilted her head and told Veronica drinks couldn't be served until we were in the air.

Veronica looked at me. She fluttered her eyes and wobbled her head. "Once we're in the air."

Moments later, with the wheels just free from the ground, Veronica punched the call button again.

"Are you going to order anything?"

Without taking my eyes from the magazine, I shook my head.

"Splendid." She bent down to paw through her purse. Her dress draped from her chest. I could see the scalloped edge of her bra. I forced myself to look past her. Through the window I watched everything I knew become meaningless. The cars and freeways, houses and buildings. They slipped into strange shapes, shrinking into points of color until I could no longer recognize their purpose. I felt a vast space tear open between me and my home. I was leaving. And either way I knew I couldn't come home the same.

None of it made me feel any better.

Veronica placed her hand on my shoulder like we were old lovers. "I want you to get a tonic. And ask for the can. We need the whole thing." I felt my pulse quicken when she said *we*. There was an unexpected excitement in *we*. Veronica put her tray table down. She put mine down too. "Me and Doug are going to enjoy ourselves." She pulled a sandwich bag from her purse. It was packed with lime wedges. Then she pulled a handle of gin from her bag. It was then that she gave me a smile so hot and terrible it made me want to do something reckless. She had the kind of mouth that made me want to transfer my savings into checking, spend it all on a weekend of empty bottles and room service.

Banking right, the sun blasted through the window. It backlit Veronica's face. The light fanned behind her head. And I felt something deep and good start to well up toward my head and I knew I was in for some kind of trouble.

Who are you? Where did you come from? I wanted to ask her. But there was no need. I already knew. She was here and she was pulling liquor from her bag. She was anybody but Lauren.

They wheeled us the ice and tonic. Veronica poured them fast. Mostly gin with a shake of tonic.

"You could be the greatest bartender in the world."

"Or the worst," she said. "First one all the way?"

I stirred at the lime in my drink. "Should we toast to something?"

"It's not that kind of drink." She tilted her glass.

We burned down the gin until the ice hit our teeth. She set up another and we raced them just as fast. She let me take my time on the third. But as a point of pride I shot that one too. I shook my glass at her. "What're you waiting for?"

"Yes, officer." And she set me up again.

Between sips her eyes rested on me with a tired stare. With liquor whiffling from her mouth she asked, "What's the worst thing you've ever done?"

I took another mouthful of gin and exhaled. "That's a little personal, Veronica."

"That's kind of the point, Doug."

I took the bottle from her and topped off my glass. A man in the row across from me watched us. He was sitting next to a lady so tired and bored she must have been his wife. He was drinking his coffee and staring. I could see he was jealous. Of the booze or me sitting with Veronica, I couldn't tell. But he had that look of a man wanting. "Never thought of bringing liquor on a plane," I said. "Who gave you this idea?"

She sipped from her cocktail straw and shook her head so her hair fell into her face. She looked at me through her bangs. "You first, Doug. Worst thing ever?"

I didn't have to search far. The gin had started working on my head and my thoughts rode off my tongue. "Years back I had to ID a victim."

Veronica leaned forward. "Like a lineup in the movies?"

"Now's not your turn. This is my story." Her eyes narrowed. I could tell she liked this kind of exchange. I waited for her to see that I was in charge. "So I was with the coroner in the hospital basement. And he takes me to the vic, pulls back the sheet—that whole thing."

Veronica touched my arm. "Were they murdered?"

"You going to let me tell it?"

She held up her hands, mocking an apology.

"We roped him out of the river. Water in his lungs. Time I got there, the man was already all examined and sewed up." I drew a line in the air, the shape of the incision. Veronica touched her collarbone. "We don't hang around for that sort of thing. So, I identify the body and the doctor leaves. It's just me and the guy. He's laying there under the light all still. And I don't know why, but looking at that drowned man I start to get angry. Something in the way he was laying there. How quiet everything was. You could hear the lights humming. And he looked young and strong enough but he wasn't moving. I don't know. I just let loose and slapped him. Right on the face. I slapped his dead face with all I had."

"What'd it feel like?" Her eyes narrowed.

"I can't remember."

"Was he cold?"

"I think so." I finished my drink in a single pull.

"You ever think hard enough about it? Enough to know why you did that?"

"No." I stared at the headrest.

"Ever done something wrong just because you could?" Veronica hid her mouth with a fist. Her eyes glinted like she'd just plucked an old memory. I wanted to know her secret.

"I guess I liked the danger of it," I said. "The doctor in the other room, being so close to trouble."

"Oh, Doug." Veronica laughed and her wide face got wider. "You have no idea how good you had it down there."

I shook my head. "It wasn't right. He never did anything to me. Far as I know, he was a good guy."

"Then why'd you do it?"

I glanced at the man across the aisle. He had finished his coffee. He was leaning into his old lady's ear, his hand rubbing her hand. I think I would have slapped him too if he looked at us again. "Hell." I shook my empty drink. I laughed a little. "I'm not sure I can—I never told anybody that story before."

Veronica's eyes kept a strange sparkle. "Your lady friend doesn't know?"

"Lauren? God, no. She doesn't have the stomach for that sort of thing." I felt dry behind my tongue. I forced myself to swallow. "I don't think she could be with a person like that."

"Jesus, you're a strange breed."

"Men?"

"Cops."

"How's that?"

"You're reckless."

I gave her a look that told her I wasn't buying.

"Think about it," she said. "When there's danger and everyone else in their right mind is running away, you guys are running toward it."

I blew the air out of my nose. She had me there. I couldn't keep clear even if I wanted. But I didn't let her know. I took the bottle and filled our glasses. We were out of tonic and were doing them straight now. And maybe that's part of why I didn't get away from it when I knew I still had time.

"Your turn," I said. "Same question." I handed her the drink. It was then that I became aware of how close we were sitting. Her forearm against my shirt sleeve. Her knees next to mine. I didn't pull away. "What's the worst thing you've ever done?"

"Honestly, I couldn't tell you, Doug." She drew long from the glass. Her chin lowered and she exhaled. "I haven't done it yet." Her head fell toward the window and it felt like she was pulling me from the aisle.

I tried to lift my drink but her hand was on top of mine.

"Let's toast," she said.

I didn't say anything.

"For tonight." She raised her glass and her eyes went big. "Stranger danger."

I wanted to tell her to stop. I wanted to tell her that Lauren was good. And that she wouldn't want me doing this, whatever we were about to do. But all I could say was, "Veronica." I said it again, even slower. "Veronica." I liked the way her name sounded coming from my mouth. There was something exotic in it. Something thrilling that couldn't be found in a name like Lauren. Veronica. Veronica. Her name was like a song.

She scribbled on a napkin. Behind her flexed hand I saw the beginning of a phone number, an area code I knew. My pulse exploded. I could feel my blood drumming in my head.

"Veronica," I said.

"Not now, Doug." She looked at me but kept writing.

My tongue felt soaked and heavy. I took another drink. "You're bad for me."

She creased the napkin and held it in front of me, teasing me, ready to pull it from my reach.

"Veronica, I can't."

"Who said I was giving it to you?"

"It wouldn't be right."

She fanned her face with the napkin. She looked like she might laugh. "Haven't you figured it out yet?"

The plane was slowing and I felt my stomach begin to rise. I listened to the engines screaming. The sound drilling in my head.

"Why? Why now?" Veronica said.

I covered my ears. "I don't know. Because she makes me take a baby aspirin."

Veronica touched the side of her neck. "If that ain't love."

The engines revved louder. My guts punching at my throat. I swallowed it down. "She calls me, every morning like clockwork. She calls and asks if I've taken my aspirin. She says it's the best thing a man my age could do. What can I say?" I wanted to smile but my mouth was sour. "She wants me around."

The booze made Veronica's eyes look big and liquid. And I honestly think she looked on me with a genuine concern. I pressed my hands tighter against my head. I imagined what Lauren was doing now. She'd already be at the airport, waiting for me at the gate. Right there in the front with a black camisole, just because I told her once—God knows when—that I liked the way it looked on her. Lauren remembers things like that.

"You don't need this in your life. You've got enough on your plate this weekend." She fished an ice cube from her drink. She positioned it between her molars and bit down. Her wet lips pouted before she blotted them with the napkin.

Of all the seats on the plane she had this one. I tried to prepare myself for Lauren. My lips shaping the words in my head.

Will you take me to be your husband?
How about we get married?
It's about time, don't you think?

But I kept running toward Veronica and her black bra. Her smooth legs. The hidden parts I wanted to see. Soon enough I'd be in the terminal clutching Lauren's familiar body. How I'd cleave to that woman. I'd put a hand on the back of her head and tell her it was alright. I'd pull her into me until her heels lift off the ground. And from that movie poster embrace I'd see Veronica waiting for her luggage. Our eyes meeting, that private moment cutting through the chaos of the airport. And with Lauren still hanging in my arms, I would know this world held more excitement and cruelty than I ever imagined.

"Give it here," I said.

Veronica shook her head before draping the napkin on the armrest between us. "You know what you're doing?"

I stuffed her number in my shirt pocket. "I'm running toward it."

My heart was punching my throat. I found it hard to take a breath. The airplane shook and the seatbelt sign came on. The engines tore louder. For the first time, I felt the sensation that we were hurtling toward the ground. My fingers curled around the end of the armrest. The plane dipped sharply and the cabin shuddered. The passengers groaned and I felt my chest tighten.

"I think I'm not well." I unbuckled my seatbelt.

Veronica laughed. "It's just a number, Doug. Don't be so dramatic." She moved her hand on mine. I got up and started for the bathroom. But before I could get to the door our flight attendant stepped into the aisle.

"Sir, the seatbelt light is on."

I tried to go past her but staggered in the aisle. She

pushed me into the nearest open seat. "Stay there," she told me. "We're landing now."

From my new seat I could see the back of Veronica's head. That wild shock of hair. I buried my eyes into my hands.

"Why?" I said. Over and over. "What's wrong with me?"

As I muttered into my lap I heard a rustling sound from the passenger next to me. Then the gentle voice of a man. "You want one?" he said. "Sucking one makes it go away."

I looked over and found myself pressed against the side of the fat man. He sat there wide and calm in the window seat, the armrest up, spilling into the aisle seat. His hands were as big as seat cushions and he rested them on his belly.

"Here," he said. He turned his hand over. A pair of pastel butter mints were centered in his palm. "This will make it better. You'll see." As I put it in my mouth he gave me the slightest of smiles. I pushed the creamy mint into my cheek. I wanted to tell him thank you. And I wanted to tell him I was sorry, for what I didn't know. But most of all I wanted to tell him that I wished he'd had my seat. It should have been him up there next to Veronica. But each time I tried to say something I found the air trapped in my lungs.

The plane rocked and a tear slipped into my mouth. I wiped my face with my sleeve.

"Have another mint," he said. "You'll see. We'll be safe and on the ground before you know it." But the thought of land just made it worse. That last gulp of air before giving up and going under.

ACKNOWLEDGMENTS[1]

I'm indebted and thankful to too many people to name them all. But I'll try my best here.

First: thank you to my parents for forcing me to go to Sunday school, where I learned the lasting power of stories. To my first writing instructors, Sydney Brown and Harold Jaffe, thank you for showing me how to read, for telling me to keep writing.

Next: to all my classmates in the San José State University MFA program, thank you for reading and grooming those early drafts. Kevin Manning and Amanda Moore, your time and care with showing me how to be a better writer. I couldn't have asked for better friends. My thesis advisors, Susan Shillinglaw, Nick Taylor, and Cathleen Miller—your collective patience and guidance—thank you. Andrew Altschul, for calling out all the bullshit. And Daniel Alarcón for teaching me not to leave any "money on the table" where the story is concerned.

Then: a million thanks to Chad Post and Kaija Straumanis for making me feel welcome when I was new in town. Thank you for introducing me to other writers and artists. Sharon Rhodes for her keen eye and kindred spirit. Peter Conners for taking a chance on me, for seeing something in my work. Thank you Rodrigo Fresán for being a friend

---

[1] *To be read frantically, with urgency, as if given at an awards ceremony and the conductor has begun playing the "will you please get off the stage now" music.*

and mentor, a writer who continually makes me want to throw my hands up and cuss at the wall—in a good way.

Always: Katie. Forever and ever. Thank you for your unending support, for showing me what grit and hard work looks like. Thank you for giving me the courage to doggedly hound my dreams. I love you.

ABOUT THE AUTHOR

Brian Wood holds an MFA in Creative Writing from San José State University. He teaches creative writing at Writers & Books. He has served as the Managing Editor of *Reed Magazine*, as well as Fiction Editor for *POST*. His work earned him an Ida Faye Sachs Ludwig Memorial Scholarship for Excellence in Creative Writing, as well as James Phelan Awards for Short Fiction and Familiar Essays.

BOA Editions, Ltd.
American Reader Series

COLOPHON

BOA Editions, Ltd., a not-for-profit publisher of poetry and other literary works, fosters readership and appreciation of contemporary literature. By identifying, cultivating, and publishing both new and established poets and selecting authors of unique literary talent, BOA brings high-quality literature to the public. Support for this effort comes from the sale of its publications, grant funding, and private donations.

• • •

The publication of this book is made possible, in part, by the special support of the following individuals:

Anonymous
June C. Baker
Gary & Gwen Conners
Joseph Finetti & Maria Mastrosimone
James Long Hale
Sandi Henschel, *in honor of Barbara Lobb*
Jack & Gail Langerak
Joe McElveney
Boo Poulin
Deborah Ronnen
Steven O. Russell & Phyllis Rifkin-Russell
William Waddell & Linda Rubel